Alabaster Sins

Alex Cristo

InAmerica Press

California, U.S.A.

Published in the United States by InAmerica Press
a division of InAmerica, Inc.
POB 2645, Valley Center, CA U.S.A.
InAmerica and colophon are registered trademarks of InAmerica, Inc.

Library of Congress Cataloging-in-Publication Data
ISBN 978-1-934613-35-1

Cristo, Alex, author.
Alabaster Sins
Alex Cristo

First U.S. Edition
[First Printing]
Copyright © 2016 by Alex Cristo
All rights reserved under International and Pan-American Copyright Conventions.

InAmerica Press website address: www.inamericapress.com
Printed in the United States of America.

Edited by Elizabeth DeGregorio

www.alexcristo.com

ALSO BY ALEX CRISTO

Crypto-Sapien
Dracula Abridged

For My Parents and Brother

Another Day at the Office

I stepped on his face with my dirty boot. The filthy ice from my sole melted down onto his cheek. I dropped the strike pamphlet, and it floated down to the wood floor next to his face like a dead leaf.

"Now that you've had a moment to think, do you remember this?" I asked, rocking the weight of my body with my boot. The wood floor creaked.

"Yes!" he said hoarsely.

"I knew you would; you just needed a moment to think," I replied. "Do you need more time to think?"

"No!"

"Good!" I helped the little man up. Dealing with these labor organizers is like trying to fish in a frozen lake: You have to keep breaking and hammering the ice until you can get to the trout. Usually they're scheming with revolutionary peasants and ambitious politicians. They're always trying to stop factory production.

I sat him in a chair and slapped away the dirt from his tunic. Dust plumed out into a cloud over his head. His three-room apartment was in much better shape than the homes of most factory workers. He used a mirror to reflect light from his tiny stove as a way of organizing, reading and corresponding. Russia was at war. The world was at war, and there were fuel shortages.

I went to the window and used my knife to cut a piece of ice hanging from the sill. I wrapped the ice in some laundry, which hung on the clothing line stretched across the room. He flinched when I reached out with the shirt.

"No, that's not what it's for." I put the ice on the red, swollen part of his face. The sudden coolness made him squint, and it began to numb his pain. I never want to bruise or break, especially the hands. Aristocracy only sees these poor bastards as a pair of hands to work, applaud and fetch.

Bruising the face only angers and emboldens the unions and peasants. It's better to have a bruise on the shoulder blade than a broken hand. A shoulder bruise doesn't keep them from working or serve as a symbol to rally behind. It just hurts!

It hurts just enough to remind them of what happened. It hurts enough to stir the imagination. A broken hand can bring sympathy, whispering and rage. I suppose it can also starve a man's family by putting him out of work. Russia doesn't want terrified workers; Russia wants calm workers, especially now that Russia is at war with Germany and the Ottomans. She cannot afford for her factories to lose production or to make do with one-handed conscripted soldiers.

"Keep that on your face for a few minutes; you need to be better for tomorrow."

"What happens tomorrow?"

"You have to go to work at the factory. Oh, were you still planning to strike?"

The little man thought of his friends and coworkers. I grabbed the ice from his face, wrapped the shirt around my hand and began to beat him on his shoulder. He hunched over, covering his head.

"Yes, I'm going to work. I'm going to work. Please, I'll go to work."

I stopped immediately.

"Good!" I said. I grabbed his hand and forced the ice back to his face. We all have our jobs to do. I still had the laundry in my hand, so I tossed it to his terrified wife and child, who were hugging each other in the corner.

This poor man would tell me everything I needed to know. He was desperate. I could taste it like sugar.

"Tell me: Where did you get these pamphlets?"

"And whom shall I say is calling?" the secretary asked.

"Don't say," I told him.

I entered through the door reserved for those of us who lack the qualities required to walk through the public entrance. It was the office of some doctor or lawyer or accountant. These businesses were usually very comfortable, with the exception of the staff's entrance.

"Very well. Wait here," the secretary instructed as he exited the room.

I knew this ambitious businessman wouldn't see me, so I stood up and followed the secretary.

I quietly pursued the stumpy man, who reminded me of a sheep. The click of his shoes echoed in the hall. Secretaries and servants generally adopt an obvious, loud walk. People of society want to know when servants are coming or going -- unless they are actually in the same room; then we must be completely silent.

The further we progressed into this building, where important people occupied the rooms, the brighter and warmer the rooms became. I hate being in these rooms. They're always so stuffy and hot.

The secretary entered an office. I put my ear to the door just in time to hear, "Well, what does he look like?"

"He's about your height. He's wearing a black coat and thick boots. He has whiskers that cover two long scars on his face; the one on the right cheek goes across the face, and the one on the left goes up and down. He has black around his eyes, and his voice is like two pieces of metal rubbing against each other."

"Get rid of him," the man sang.

"Yes, sir."

I hid behind a corner and waited until the secretary had gone. Then I entered the office.

"Who the hell are you?" the man protested.

"I'm sorry, sir. I'm on a schedule and couldn't wait."

"I am very busy, so if you don't mind, please leave," he prattled on until I held up the pamphlet.

"Sorry to interrupt you, sir. Where did you get this?" I asked.

He was silent. These people are only silent when they are scared or confused. He was both.

"I don't know what you're talking about," he answered.

"Perhaps you need a moment to think."

I left the building and walked onto the street. Two other agents of the special guards were waiting to follow me. These were my men. I could intimidate them and trust them.

I had a terrible headache from going into the factory worker's house and the businessman's office. I always get headaches. It must be the heat in those places. I walked out into the cold air. My eyes stung, and I was annoyed that I had to walk all the way across the city twice.

My men and I climbed into our carriage and rode it to the address that the businessman had given me. Our destination was a small bakery. It was a cover for labor agitators. We stopped around the corner.

I reached under my coat and pulled out my metal pipe. My headache had only worsened, and I was anxious to get this job finished. I tried to take a moment to clear my head and stop the shaking. The agent behind me bumped into my shoulder, and I rapped him on his arm with my pipe. I wasn't frightened; he just startled me.

I put the pipe under my sleeve and walked into the bakery.

"May I help you?" the baker asked.

"Shut up!" I told him. As I sprang over the counter, I grabbed some bread slices and threw them at the baker as hard as I could. Then I forced my way behind the display counter.

I grabbed the top of an understocked cabinet and pulled it down to the floor. The clay jars that held the ingredients shattered onto the floor seconds before being smashed by the wooden cabinet. There was one jar with four eggs, a small tin of sugar and a medium-sized container of flour. The impact made the flour waft up into the air and left a chalky taste in my mouth.

The two special guards stumbled behind me over the broken containers and slippery floor. I coughed and tried to wave the flour out of my face. Then, using my shoulder, I forced open the door hidden behind the cabinet.

Inside the hidden room were two men. One man with a vest was hunched over the desk with a candle; the other was by the window, using the sunlight to read. They were thin, weedy-looking men with sunken cheeks and dark circles around their eyes. They tied cords over their tunics as belts. I rushed to the desk and grabbed the first man by his coat, throwing him to the ground.

I began to beat him with my pipe and kick him with my boot. Every time I made contact with the screaming man, the force of the impact ran through the pipe and up my arm, making my headache worsen. In turn, the pain made me swing harder, which just caused my head more pain. I beat him and beat him and beat him.

The man by the window tried to run past me, but the two guards grabbed him and threw him down. The blood caused the flour to form into a gum that stuck to my coat.

After I had finished with my metal pipe, I told the two guards to take the men on the floor to the truck and turn them over for more questioning. Questioning doesn't involve a lot of questions. It usually involves ropes and knives and iron rods.

I was questioned once. My arms were tied behind my back, and I was hung from my legs for hours. They kicked me, electrocuted me and raped me with a metal pipe. When I begged them to stop, they put a gun in my face and pulled the trigger. The mock execution is always the worst.

My joints still hurt from those questions, and every time I walk or beat someone, I can feel it all through my body.

I stayed behind and stood by the window to cool down and stop the dizziness. Why do I always have to fight the nausea? Must be the heat in these places. Once I caught my breath, I tried to look around the room.

The desk had pens, paper and a cup of urine, which they used as invisible ink. I took a handful of papers and writing supplies and carried it out to the cart. I walked through the bakery to the door where I saw the rest of the papers and pamphlets being loaded into the cart. I slapped my gloves against my chest to clear away the flour glued to my coat with the men's blood.

Some of the flour was still floating in the air like a ghost. There was a small jar of flour on the floor that had not been broken. I kicked it with my boot and watched it shatter against wall.

Now they have nothing.

Time for a Drink

Workers and peasants. I hate them all. Alone in a room with me, everyone is the same. Station and integrity are useless unless people are around to see it. Tomorrow the worker will be just as pathetic, and that politician will be just as respected. I wish I could interrogate a nobleman outside. I am not a noble or a peasant. I am just a boot with a knife in it.

After I turned the agitators over for more questioning, I was finally finished for the day. I decided to go have a drink and then see my friend the priest. I entered my local tavern and stomped my boots. The way people react to the sound can betray more about their intentions than they realize. If a man casually looks up and then returns to his drink, he's unimportant. If a man doesn't react, he's dumb. If a man darts his eyes at me, I take note and never turn my back to him. Today there was such a man with darting eyes seated in the corner.

I grabbed my usual drink with one hand and slapped the tavern owner on the back with the other. Random actions can be enough to confuse or even postpone a possible attack, especially if they think you have friends to back you up. Men with darting eyes seem to panic when caught unprepared.

I wandered around the bar and touched the shoulder of a stranger to give anyone watching me the impression that I had friends here. I didn't. Then I sat down in a corner and stared at the man with the darting eyes. They say you can see into a man's soul by looking into his eyes. Hopefully this idiot believes that and sees my eyes. His confused glances gave something away: He had a partner.

I spotted his partner out of the corner of my eye. He was an older man with a fur coat and a mustache with two perfect hooks on the ends. Under his dirty coat, he had on an imported suit made of bright silk. He wrung his expensive gloves out with his bare hands.

Any fool could see through such a lazy disguise.

Are these men assassins? Something didn't feel right. The man with the darting eyes makes sense; I'm being watched, tracked or cornered. But this silk bastard doesn't make sense. My first instinct was to run, lead them down a blind corner and smash their hands with my pipe.

I finished my drink in one gulp and flipped the empty glass around my fingers. While I was constantly looking toward the man with darting eyes, I put the glass on its side and pointed the open end at the silk bastard. I never looked at him. It was a quiet way to let him know I saw him.

I waited for him to make the next move. The tavern owner saw what was going on and scratched his nose at me. I responded by dusting off my shoulder, and he returned the knife to his pocket and continued sweeping with his broom.

The silk bastard looked toward the man with the darting eyes and nodded. The man with the darting eyes stood and slowly made his way toward me. He should have his hands broken. I continued to stare at him as he approached me.

"May I join you?"

I could tell by his walk that he was frightened. He took small steps and kept his body turned to the side. I would be surprised if he had ever made a fist in his life.

"We are not here to harm you," he said weakly.

"How comforting."

"All I'm supposed to do is hand you this." He retrieved a letter from his coat pocket and presented it to me.

"Something wrong with using the post?" I asked.

"If you don't take it, I'm supposed to write this." He took his finger, ran it over his coat to make it wet and drew a box with the number 28 inside. I wiped away the symbol on the table and took the letter, still keeping my eyes on the silk bastard across the room.

This code was used by superiors to inform agents in the field that they were to be trusted. It is supposed to be an all-clear signal. I have never seen an actual superior use this code, but I did see it used once to bring in an agent for questioning.

"Who's it from?" I asked

"The tsar," he replied.

The claim was so ridiculous that I almost laughed.

I immediately stood up to leave, and the man with the darting eyes followed me. He caught up to me and swung his knee into my stomach.

I fell down, then reached into my coat and grabbed my pipe. I brought the pipe down with all my force onto his right hand. I heard a few bones crack, and he began to scream. He threw me against the wall and stuffed my scarf into my mouth. The impact caused pain to radiate through my joints and made my headache scream. He continued to punch me until I collapsed.

The silk bastard stood, grabbed his cane and sat at my table. He began to put on his gloves. The darting eyes man held me against the floor with his arms.

"Was that necessary?" he asked. I could see his very expensive suit under the old coat. He began to light his cigarette, placing it into a black holder so that it wouldn't get his gloves dirty with ash. He had a bright gold lighter that looked heavy. "Why did you hurt his hand? All he wanted to do was give you your new orders."

"I don't know what you're talking about," I told him. Orders come from my superiors, never from men dressed as fancy whores. I have heard stories of assassins using this very same strategy.

"I will say, my little boy, I like your…thoroughness," he said, laughing to himself. I suppose he had just made a joke. "Why don't we go to your superiors and get this straightened out? Let him go."

Once I was released, I ran as fast as I could out the door and down the street. They didn't try to follow me.

The Church

Outside, I circled the block until I was sure that no one was following me. Next to a large thundering factory was a small church. I entered the side door. The smell of candles, incense and machine grease made my eyes water. The colored windows shined with the light breaking through the glowing black smoke of the factory stacks.

The priest was sweeping the corner with a straw broom. The soot and black ash from the factory blew right through the walls and over the entire floor, the icons and the altar. The father constantly tried to sweep out the ash, but it was impossible -- the factory expelled too much darkness for any man to clean. His broom had been worn to one side and was black as though it had been dipped in tar.

He saw me, threw his broom against the wall and stomped over.

"I told you: You can't come in here until you renounce your evil ways," he whispered angrily. He was a short old man. His frizzy gray beard was stained with black soot from the factory.

"I want to talk to you," I told him.

"Go to the back," he said. He picked up his broom and bucket. I left the church and walked to the back from the alley where they dumped waste and spoiled garbage. The father opened a window hatch and tossed the waste from his bucket to the alley. The fine dust plumed into a black fog that rose to my waist. He pulled up a wooden crate for me to sit on before he propped the window open with his broom.

"Until you accept the Lord into your heart and reject your sinful ways, you will never have peace or happiness. I don't know what else there is I can tell you."

"I still get headaches," I said.

"You get headaches because your blood is poisoned with the evil things you do."

"It's just the heat." I put my hand into the black cloud and began to stir up a tornado.

"Why do you keep coming here? What purpose does it serve? Look at you. You have blood on your coat. You come here fresh from your sins."

"It's just flour," I told him. "I was doing my job. I serve the tsar. Actually, you and I have the same vocation. The tsar is the head of the church, and I am part of the tsar's special police force."

The priest laughed mockingly. "So you believe it's God's wish that you hurt people?"

"In a way, yes. I perform the tsar's will. The tsar performs God's will."

"Do you get your orders directly from the tsar?"

"No."

"Do you get your orders directly from his subordinate?"

"No."

"From paper written by his own hand?"

"There is a chain of command we follow."

"You get your orders through men, and men are fallible. Through these orders, you do terrible things to people. And it has poisoned your soul."

"It's just the heat."

Audience with the Tsar

I weaved my way through the streets, back and forth, in and out of several blocks. I wanted to make sure no one was following me. I recognized the silk bastard from somewhere. He was one of the tsar's administrators or counselors or something. Maybe he was a noble.

They constantly sent people out to test your loyalty. If you failed the test, you just became another little person at the end of a stick. That silk bastard knew that I couldn't touch him. Just like any dog that turns on its handler, I would quickly be put down.

I backtracked and circled a few times, making my way back to the Okhrana Special Guard main office.

I passed by the vendor on the street who sold watches. He kept them on an old blanket and spent most of the day rearranging them. They were worthless; most of them didn't work at all, and the ones that did couldn't keep time accurately. They were half the price of watches that worked and a third of the price of watches that didn't. Most people couldn't tell time and just wore watches as ornaments. They were gifts to firstborn males to welcome them into low-caste manhood. Working-class fools stared at these broken watches for hours, coveting them and trying to learn to tell time. They don't need them. The foreman tells them when to go back to work.

I found my way to my superior's office. The clerk lifted his head and looked over his glasses at me. He was a short, annoying man who wore the best clothing that his bribes could afford. I gave him rent sometimes to keep myself out of the more uncomfortable assignments. But lately I hadn't bothered to bribe him. All the assignments were uncomfortable.

"Should I go in now?" I asked.

"Wait a moment," he replied condescendingly. He was arranging some papers and wanted to make me wait. People loved to make you wait. I began to feel the heat from the room melt away the cold around me. I felt dizzy and disoriented.

The clerk finally looked up from his desk. "Go in now," he told me.

I entered the room. The walls were made from dark-stained wood. The light was too dim to do any work other than drinking and blowing smoke out of a fat mouth. I walked toward the giant desk.

My superior was standing while someone else sat in his chair. I couldn't see who it was because of the low light.

"Hello there, my little boy." It was the same silk bastard with the cigarette holder. He lifted his boots onto the desk and smiled at me. Without the coat, I could see the fine tailored suit from Germany.

"You must apologize to him," my superior instructed me.

"Apologize for what?" I asked, tightening my fist.

My superior slammed his fist on the table. "How dare you, you pathetic bastard! This is the Grand Duke! Nephew to the tsar himself! You will apologize for your disrespectful tone toward him this instant, or I will have you in front of a firing squad."

"He was in a disguise; I didn't know who he was," I protested.

"That is inconsequential," my superior responded.

"Open the door," the silk bastard ordered. My superior trotted around the desk and flung open the door. After the door was open and everyone could hear me being humiliated, they continued to scream at me.

It took me almost two minutes before I could vomit out an apology.

"I apologize for my disrespect, sir. Please forgive me." It felt as though I was biting my inner cheek with every word.

"I am to give you this. It has the special seal of the tsar himself, and it is for your eyes only." He took it and threw it over the table, watching it as it slide over onto the floor. "Oh, that was too hard of a throw, wasn't it, my little boy?"

I bent over to pick up the letter, and he slammed his hand on the dark desk.

"Wasn't it?" he yelled.

"Yes, it was, sir." I was speaking softly, but it was all I could manage.

"You must treat the tsar's summons with respect, you bastard. Don't let it go on the floor!" the silk bastard continued.

The seal had already been opened. This fop could have easily opened and resealed the letter without detection, but he wanted me to know that he could look, and there was nothing I could do about it. I was so angry that I couldn't even read it; I was lightheaded and could feel the pipe beneath my coat.

"It is a summons; you are to meet the tsar in person," the silk bastard informed me. "That is a very big honor. He is the most powerful man in the world. His reign covers one-third of the Earth. Few beggars like you get such an honor. For a special assignment, I presume? What kind of assignment do you think he has in mind, my little boy?"

"I don't know, sir."

"Well, that doesn't surprise me. Grab my coat and follow me," he said, putting his cigarette out on the floor. The urge to gouge out his eyes overcame me. I picked up his coat.

"What's your name?" my superior asked me in a whisper as I passed him. I pretended I didn't hear him. This was only the third or fourth time that I had ever seen him.

I followed the silk bastard outside and watched him get into a very plush motorcar. It was big, long and shined to resemble a black mirror. The reflections displayed an image of the street -- glossy and curved, like satin ice.

He held out his hand for his coat. Once he grabbed it from me, he pointed down to signal that I was to ride next to the driver. The front part of the motorcar was not covered. After being in the hot, stuffy office, I didn't mind. I needed to cool off and be alert.

The Winter Palace. It was like a white cliff cresting over the city. It was still and cold.

We pulled up to the outer gate and were immediately approached by two guards with rifles. The silk bastard gave the guard a cream-colored piece of paper, and we were instantly waved onto the palace grounds. Once we were inside the outer gate, the air became tighter.

We passed one of the main entrances and turned a corner along the side of the palace. Ahead of me was the Neva River. I could smell the freshly painted walls. Even the unseen sides of the palace were freshly painted. I could practically taste the white marble and the green paint. We pulled up to a covered ramp, and the silk bastard shoved his paper into another guard's face.

I jumped down from the top of the cab. The silk bastard pushed his cane and coat into my chest and snapped his fingers, ordering me to follow him. I followed but didn't look up. I didn't want to draw attention to myself with my own darting eyes. Everything was so clean and crisp.

The guards approached me, and I showed them my official papers.

"Are you armed?" one of the guards asked.

"Yes," I answered. I took out my knife, my pipe and my rope. He put them on the floor against the wall and began to search me for any other weapons.

I entered the palace, looking down at the ground. The floors were polished to a reflection; it was like walking on a looking glass. The doors and walls were as tall as fifty men. They were painted with brilliant colors that I had never seen before. Gold was everywhere -- it was on the ceiling and on the floor. It seemed to grow up the wall and marble like ivy.

We walked in a line. The silk bastard led the group, twirling his cane. Behind him were the servants and attendants. They were never allowed to walk in front of someone of a high station. Behind the servants were two palace guards. The guards stomped the exact same way, like a second-rate ballet.

I followed behind the guards since I occupied the lowest position. The statue in the corner was more important than me. I was at the mercy of everyone inside and outside of this gilded bear den.

The ceiling was so far away that every footstep was multiplied by hundreds of echoes. It was a hollow and tinny echo that hurt my ears.

I saw an arrangement of plants in the corner. I had never seen anything like them before. The trunks were long and thin, and they had exotic leaves that grouped together to make fans. The leaves were shaped like scimitars. They were lined up in a row out of the way of everything else. Almost forgotten.

"Those are palm trees, my little boy. They only grow in the tropics." He laughed and added, "As though you know what that means. They only grow in lands where the temperature is warm all year round, toward the center of the Earth. Our country is at the top of the Earth, you know."

He stopped the entire group of people. "The Earth is round, by the way." He walked back toward me and shoved his pointy cane into my stomach. "I have ten palm trees, my little boy. How many do you have?" He turned and continued to walk, laughing and twirling his cane.

We went on for miles. Every room had a doorway with an arch of gold. All the doorways were open. You could see straight down further than the eyes could focus. Rooms after rooms after rooms.

Even the portraits and statues took no notice of me as we passed them. Everything in this palace was above everything else. After what seemed like an hour of walking down the hall, a short, angular man with white gloves came toward me.

"Are you he?" he asked, examining me.

"Yes, this is him," the silk bastard replied as he shoved the paper into the short man's chest. He took the paper with his gloved hands, looked it over and then turned back to me.

"Come with me," he said, turning and strutting down the hall.

I was led to the tsar's personal reception office for public audiences. There was a chair placed in the middle of the giant room. The man with the white gloves took my coat and sat me down. I felt like an island in the middle of this giant sea of gold and wood.

The chair had a soft velvet cushion. The frame was so firm and sturdy. Not one creak. The wood was so intricately designed that it must have grown out of the ground in the shape of a chair. The cream paint looked to be mixed with sugar and flour. The chair was the nicest and most powerful thing I have ever touched in my life.

"The tsar wishes to speak to him alone," the man with the white gloves told the silk bastard.

"Excuse me? There must be some mistake," he demanded. The man with the white gloves took the coat and cane from me and herded the silk bastard out of the room. I could hear him stomping all the way to the door. Then I was alone in the room.

The bottom half of the walls were cut and carved from fine-smelling wood and were as tall as a man. The top half of the walls held portraits of men with facial hair so fine that it looked like braided steel.

The tsar's desk was made from heavy wood that was decorated with gold and bright, shining paint. It was as plush as the women in the portraits looking down at me.

Through the thick door in front of me, I could hear faint footsteps. They were like heartbeats, approaching faster and faster. I couldn't stop myself from blinking. There was a rumbling from the door behind the desk. Then the door swung open, and two attendants entered. They surveyed me and the rest of the room.

When the tsar entered, I stood up immediately.

The tsar was short. He ruled all of Russia, one-third of the world, and was only as tall as the attendants who followed him. He was a very slight and wiry man, which I could see even through his impressive uniform. His clothes, though perfectly tailored, slumped like wet sheets on a clothing line across his shoulders. He had a flattened nose that turned up at the end. His blue eyes were so vibrant that they were glowing. He had a thick golden beard under his mustache, which he obsessively brushed with the back of his hand.

He was rubbing his index finger with his thumb as he made his way directly to the desk. The attendants followed behind him nervously. They performed a ballet of movements in seating the tsar: One attendant held the chair out and pushed it in when the tsar sat, while the other brought paper, pens, notes and bells from the edge of the desk to within the tsar's reach.

It was an amazing orchestration of complex movements. The tsar would reach for something, one attendant would bring the object closer, and the other would arrange everything else accordingly. After what seemed to be half an hour of adjusting and reaching, the tsar was finally ready.

"I have never seen you," the tsar said in a thin and nasal voice. The attendant behind me tapped my shoulder subtly to signal that I was to speak.

"No, your majesty."

"Family man?" the tsar questioned. The distance between us forced me to strain to hear him; he had a very weak voice.

The attendant tapped my shoulder. But I felt like they saw me as a puppet, and I didn't answer. The tsar took little notice and never looked directly at me. He turned his attention to sifting through papers and having his two men move things around on his desk.

The tsar continued, "You are positioned in my special guard and have cultivated a positive appraisal and…and a reputation from your superiors, who have briefed me on the exploits and competencies that don't seem to find their way onto records and reports."

There was a long silence. The attendant was now tapping my shoulder like a woodpecker. I didn't know what to say, and since I knew that saying nothing is always a better option, stayed silent.

The tsar set his pen down with a tap. The room froze. As he looked up at me, I could see the beard and mustache move out of the corner of my eye. I knew what it meant. I never dared to look into his eyes.

The tsar looked at the man over his shoulder and nodded. He rubbed his finger with his thumb again as the entire staff exited the room.

The tsar leaned back in his chair for a moment, inspecting his finger and considering. Then he pressed his back into the chair, the medals and chords on his uniform swinging into each other like hands on a broken watch.

"What do you know of the man called Rasputin?"

"Only rumors, your majesty. He's something like a holy man with a...notorious reputation," I said.

"Very good. Notorious. Notorious," he repeated as he stood up. The chair was pushed backwards when his legs locked, and it slid five feet backwards due to the heavy polish on the floor. He began to pace along the walls of the room. His footsteps sounded like the chambering of a bullet into a rifle.

I kept my eyes forward. I could hear him walk, sounding as if he was working through something in his mind. His clothes and medals jingled against each other.

The slow footsteps behind me caused me to shiver. I instinctively closed my eyes, waiting for a gun to be fired at the back of my head or a knife to go through my throat. After a few laps, he returned to the front of his desk. He stood straight and still without fidgeting or swaying.

"You will be pulled away from your current assignments. Your new duty consists of two objectives. You will follow the man known as Rasputin. First you will act as a passive, protective force and personal guard. No harm is to come to this man. While you are performing this duty, you will detail everything he does and everywhere he goes. You report directly to me and only to me. Nothing is to happen to this man! Is this understood?"

"Yes, your majesty. Protect the man Rasputin, and report to you on his movements. To you and only you."

"Very good. You are to start immediately. He is in the hospital. You will receive the location outside. There are guards posted on him now, and they are waiting for you."

"Yes, your majesty," I said. Before he rang the bell on the desk, he looked at me out of the side of his eye for the first time and said, "Very good!"

The door swung open, and the attendants helped the tsar exit the room, which seemed to take hours. "Very good," he repeated as the door closed behind him.

I was alone again. The man with the white gloves entered and handed me the address I needed to find Rasputin. Then he took out a handkerchief and began furiously slapping and wiping the nice chair I was on. He brought the cloth to his face and was revolted by the smell. He held his handkerchief out as far as his arms could reach and shooed me out of the room. He handed the handkerchief to an attendant.

"Burn this!" he demanded in a nasal voice.

Outside, I saw the silk bastard waiting for me. His ears were perked up as he sniffed around me like a dog.

"What did he say?" he demanded.

"I'm only supposed to report to the tsar himself," I told him as I collected my pipe and other weapons.

"Is that so?" he asked, slowly putting his gloves on. "I will take you back to your tavern." He passed his coat and cane from the attendant to me and marched down the hallway. He watched me out of the corner of his eye to be sure that I was following him.

We exited the palace, and I handed him his coat. As I was about to climb up to sit by the driver, I heard him knock on the outer door with his cane.

"Ride with me inside," he said, opening the door. As I climbed in, I slipped the pipe from my coat to my sleeve and palmed it.

It was very cramped inside. We sat facing each other, and our knees were touching. A lady must usually sit here because there was a heavy scent of perfume in the cushion.

"What did you think about meeting the tsar in person?" he asked, clicking the cigarette extender between his teeth. "Few men in the world have had such a privilege. Even kings and queens can't always get an audience."

"It was an honor."

"Yes, it was. Yes, it was. What did you think of him?" he asked, smiling at me.

"He is a great man."

"Oh, he certainly is. But he can be a little...you know..." He trailed off as he leaned closer to me, hoping to draw something out of me. He was testing my loyalty or trying to familiarize himself with me.

"A great honor, sir," I said. He laughed and leaned back, realizing I wouldn't be that easy to charm.

"Yes, it was. You know, even a great man like the tsar needs all of us to do our parts and help. Let me give you an example. The tsar eats his own food. No one can eat it for him. The food keeps him strong and fit to rule justly. But the cook doesn't bring it to him. He gives it to a server who gives it to an attendant who gives it to a taster. The taster digests a piece of the food to make sure it hasn't been poisoned. I do the same thing with information. So it is for the tsar's own well-being that you let me make sure the information you are giving him won't poison him. This is your duty. Do you understand?"

I looked around for a moment and felt relieved that I wouldn't have to use my pipe. I rang the bell to let the driver know to stop.

"This is where I stop," I said as I exited the cab. I began to walk down an alley.

"Call me 'sir,' you dirty beggar!" he yelled, causing everyone to turn and look at me.

"This is where I stop, sir," I said. I turned my back to him and took out my watch. Although the silk bastard was secure in his superiority, he sounded desperate. I could taste it like sugar. He knocked his cane on the side of his car repeatedly.

I didn't even see them coming. I was tackled from behind and hit over the head. I don't know how many there were kicking me. That's why the silk bastard wanted me to ride in the back. His guards could ride in the front and beat me. I didn't try to get up. There was no point. I stopped trying long ago. It's easier just to take it.

I don't remember how long I was out for. I was robbed of everything but my pipe. My watch was gone. They kicked me so hard that my entire left arm was numb, and I was missing two teeth.

Keep the Windows Open

I walked slowly back to headquarters. I wanted to get this silk bastard's limp out of my system before I returned. Walking with a limb shows weakness, and it can get me more beatings. I limped for almost a year after I was questioned. I returned home to get some money and a drink of water. The pain and stiffness was beginning to set in.

When I walked back to headquarters, I entered the building and waited until no one was watching. I had to endure the pain to hide the limp. Then I climbed the stairs to the top floor. The top floor is where all the paperwork is found. People file, fill out forms and process requests. The most useful people upstairs are those in the map room.

A good map is better than a gun. Maps can do so many valuable things, from monitoring people's everyday habits to charting avenues of escape. If you know that there are only two streets that can lead to a certain location, you are ten times more likely to be ahead of the other guy. I have sold many of them on the street for more money than I make in a month.

I found one of the men in the map room sharpening his pencils.

"I need a new map," I told him.

"Location, scale and radius," the map man said, running his sharpening blade along the tip of his black pencil.

"Here is the address for the center point." I handed him a piece of paper with Rasputin's address. "I need about three miles extending outward. It can't be too big."

"Yes," he said, filling out a work form. I grabbed his pencil from his hand before he could write anything.

"I need this one off the books," I told him. Then I handed him his pencil back with some crumpled money from my boot. "And I need it quickly."

Keeping this assignment off the books and following the tsar's orders has already cost me two teeth, a numb arm and the last of my money.

"I think I can arrange that." He put the money in his pocket and returned the form neatly to its place in the folder.

Once I walked into the street, a breeze hit my right shoulder. The open air felt good, especially after being indoors with those kind of people.

Every class exists in its own temperature. I think aristocrats are unable to keep their own bodies warm and must live in a furnace. I always kept the windows open in my room. The icy steam from outside cauterized any smell and kept the mice away. I never get cold at night, only in the morning.

I was hungry and didn't want to make the walk back to my part of the city on an empty stomach. I decided to pay a visit to a woman I knew. As I made my way up the staircase, I could smell the dead rats under the wood. I knocked at the door. She forced a smile and took my coat. No matter how many times I entered or how long I stayed, I never felt at home. I told her to make me something to eat, and she tried to keep from touching me on her way to the kitchen.

"Keep the windows open," I told her. I don't know how many times I have to say it.

"Sorry, I was changing and forgot to open it back," she said. I jerked the window out, and it slammed against the wall. I grabbed a chair and sat in the breeze's line of fire, hoping to cool off.

She heard the slam and came over, trying to hug me from behind. Her body forced my metal pipe into my side. It reminded me how painful it was when they questioned me. I used the back of my arms to push her off of me. She fell into the cupboard. The dishes and cups rattled like sleigh bells. The sound made me so angry that I wanted to close the window and throw her through it.

I was in a room alone with the tsar today. Few men can claim that. Men of ambition would kill to be where I was today, even that silk bastard, the Grand Duke. This Rasputin must be important to get such personal attention from the tsar. Maybe all the things they say about him are true.

After I finished eating, I took her into the bedroom.

When I left, I closed the door behind me and wandered back to the street. I was happy with this new assignment because it kept me off the front lines. Being assigned to fight was being assigned to die.

Report to Duty

I entered the hospital with my official papers already in my hand. I approached the two guards stationed outside a closed door. As they checked my documents against their book, I noticed that they were unsettled. Something had happened. They handed my papers back.

"What do you want us to do?" the short one asked.

"Stay here. I'll be relieving you when he's discharged. Is he in there?"

"Yes. His nurse has black hair and a scar on her neck. The doctor is short and bald. We've already talked to the police -- they should stay out of your way. They placed him in a special wing. Even though they're crowded, the hospital was forced to isolate him."

"Why did they separate him?" I asked the guard.

"He was frightening the other patients."

"Does he have a plague?"

"No, he was scaring them with his screaming and ramblings," the guard said carefully.

"What was he saying?"

"I'd rather not repeat it, sir," he told me, making the sign of the cross.

"What happened to him?" I asked. "How was he injured?"

"A woman walked up to him with a butcher knife and carved into him from his chest to his pelvis. The nurse told me that he was holding his intestines in with his hand."

"And he survived?"

"Yes."

"How could he survive that?"

"The nurse thought he was the devil," the tall one said, smiling. "They say he makes women faint just from walking behind them. Do you know anything about him?"

"Don't ask so many questions," I told them. A nurse entered his room with paper and ink. After a few moments, I heard a thump, and then she emerged with a sealed envelope and slammed the door. She stomped down the hall.

"You there," I said.

"Yes?" she answered as she turned around.

"I'm a member of the detail that is guarding the man in that room, and I was wondering if I could have a look at that letter. Here, allow me to show you my credentials." Before I could reach into my pocket, she handed me the envelope.

"You can be a German spy for all I care. How dare he speak to me that way?" She clearly resented Rasputin and was pleased to be able to participate in any small act of defiance.

I looked at the sealed letter. It was addressed to the tsar. Why is this man sending personal letters to the tsar himself? This dirty peasant from Siberia is corresponding with the greatest man in the world? I took out a small leather pouch from my jacket's inner right pocket. I opened the flap and pulled out a thin metal instrument. It was round with a cleft that ran down the entire tool.

I held the sealed letter in between my fingertips and squeezed. While flexing the envelope, I was able to separate the sealed flap from the side. I inserted my instrument into the opening and down the throat of the letter. I pushed down on the tool and inserted the corner of the letter inside the envelope into the cleft. Once it was secure, I began to roll the metal rod between my fingers.

The sealed letter rolled onto the tool like rope on a winch. I pulled the note out and unwrapped it. The letters were big and clumsy. The ink was smeared from his hands, and the note appeared to be furiously composed, with the words trailing off and down the side.

I squinted my eyes and read the letter.

A terrible storm cloud lies over Russia.
Disaster, grief, murky darkness and no light.
A whole ocean of tears…there is no counting them, and so much blood.
The disaster is great, the misery infinite.
-Rasputin.

I rolled the letter back into my tool and into the sealed envelope. I handed it back to the nurse.

"Madness, isn't it?"

"You read it?" I asked.

"He read it to me. Then he told me how intimate he was with the tsarina."

"Intimate?" I asked. She made a vulgar motion with her hand. "Did he say what the note meant?"

"It was a premonition of the war, he said. It came to him in a vision."

"Thank you," I told her. She put the letter in her pocket and returned to her work.

I peeked through an open door into his room. He was sitting on a chair looking out the window. He had two mattresses with extra sheets and pillows. Even though he was sitting, I could see that he was tall. His hair was coarse and wild. His frail, thin frame was hunched over, and he was holding his chest.

Suddenly he turned around and looked right at me. His eyes hit me. Those eyes looked through me, at me, around me and in front of me. They were blue and terrible, like knots of wood in a dead tree.

I quickly ducked my head away from the window. I could feel him looking at me through the wall. His long dirty beard and gaunt face hovered over the elongated fingers that grabbed his chest. I tried to escape down the hall. I still felt his eyes glaring at me, tracking me.

I returned home after I posted two guards and a watchman to keep a journal of any movements. Rasputin wasn't due to leave the hospital for a few days. I could rest and heal.

I removed my boots, opened the window and got into bed. I'm always hot. Ever since I was a boy, it's been impossible to cool down in the evenings.

"Always close the window!" That old man would always scream. Ever since I was a baby. "The girls and the customers need it warm!"

The sun never hit my one-room flat. It was permanently in the shadow of the surrounding buildings. The factories and smoke left a smog over the entire block. I don't feel cool until the mornings. The frigid morning air always wakes me hours before I need to be up. Then I spend the early morning trying to warm myself.

I made a habit of keeping inventory of my pockets. In my right front jacket pocket, I kept my official papers and documents. They were folded into quarters individually and stacked on top of each other. I also kept a small bundle of rope. This is for tying, strangle or carrying. In my jacket's left inner pocket, I kept a knife. It was fifteen centimeters with a black handle. I always make sure to know exactly how much money I have in my pockets.

Under my coat and jacket, in my belt, I kept a metal pipe I took from one of the factory garbage heaps. It was thin enough to fit in my hand and heavy enough to be very painful. While I was qualified to use a firearm, agents didn't carry them. They were too expensive to buy, and the department stopped issuing them after the war started. Agents were required to report every other week for target practice until the war caused bullet shortages. The pipe was usually more than enough. I was questioned once with a pipe.

Rasputin lived alone in an apartment on Gorochowaya. That is very luxurious for a priest. He must be very important to the tsar. He is rumored to have hypnotic powers and thought to be able to broker deals with the devil. From what I understand, he is something of an oddity, and hostesses love having him at parties for a cheap thrill.

I always hate the first two weeks of guarding a civilian. Every place they go and every face they see is completely new to me. No matter where you guard them, they're always in their small village. For most people, their village is made up of their home, their work and their tavern. Most people live their entire lives in four rooms. Except me -- I live in everyone else's rooms. I'm always a stranger in a village of idiots.

Rasputin should be less of a burden because he knows we're here to protect him. He probably won't be very mobile at all, considering his knife wound.

I pulled my coat over my face to heat up my ears. I was very thirsty but couldn't summon the strength to find my water pitcher. I didn't think there was any water in it, but it made me feel better to think that there was. It became harder to breathe, so I tried to inhale in small amounts. Then I opened my mouth, which exposed my face to the chill of the outside world. The cold air stung my gums where my teeth were kicked out. I was too tired to close my mouth.

Still thinking about water from the pitcher, I wondered what the color purple smells like. I want to grab the color purple and roll it into a ball so that I can take bites out of it. I should put glass on the inside of my clothes so people can't see me. Then I can replace the panes of glass with my shoes until there is no more sawdust on the floor...

I awoke flexing every muscle. My teeth hurt from clamping my jaw. I rushed to close the window. I buried myself in my coat and blanket. The air was thin under the cloth and fur, and it became harder to breath.

I pulled back the cover and inhaled. The cold air froze my throat and chest. My lungs felt like they were trying to escape my body. I coughed and gasped.

At headquarters, I put in a request for two men to help me watch Rasputin. They were both young and capable. I could also turn them over to the firing squad based on things I knew about them, which made them more anxious to keep me happy. If a person is too clean, you can't trust them.

I turned in my request sheet. The clerk took it and quickly looked over it.

"You must fill it out completely," he said, without looking up at me.

"I can't," I told him. He looked up at me with his annoyed, pointed face.

"What do you mean, you can't? You can read, can't you? You can answer simple questions, can't you?" He threw the paper back at me, and it floated to the floor.

"I can't because I'm under special orders. Now process it."

"Get out of here," he demanded, returning his attention to the papers. He was hassling me to get his rent. I decided I better pay him before I became too angry to control myself. I pulled out some money and put it next to his inkwell.

"More!" he said without looking up. I added to the pile and stood in silence. With no other word, I assumed the deal was done. I picked up the request from the floor and handed it to him. He grabbed it from me with a clap.

"And an apology," he added.

I waited for the initial breeze of anger to calm before I turned around. It took me almost a full minute to spit out my words.

"I apologize," I said through my teeth.

"Sir," he said, looking right at me.

"I apologize, sir." I was so angry that I became dizzy.

"Don't let it happen again. You may go now." He flicked his wrist at me and went on with his work. The people who don't deserve respect still make you fake it for them.

I stomped upstairs to the map room. The map man was hovering over a drafting table, carefully transferring street information. Others around him were doing the same, and the room was silent and still.

"Do you have something for me?" I asked him.

"Not yet. Check back later," he said.

"How long?"

"It'll be done when it is done. Don't rush me," he snapped.

As I was on my way to my new assignment, I stopped by my young newspaper reader. This young man with glasses read the newspaper to me. I could read it myself, but it would take too long, and I would not understand a good deal of the words. He loved to read the papers but could seldom afford them. He would explain the politics to me, and I would listen quietly. He also somehow collected a great deal of useful information by just reading and talking with other people. There is a comforting calmness to someone telling you everything.

I didn't have to pay him money or food for the reading. All I had to do was supply him with pens, ink and blank paper. I would give him half-printed labor pamphlets or stationary stolen from the clerk's desk. He was a writer of some sort. I think I remember someone somewhere telling me his writing was good. It doesn't really matter how good they are. Who cares about stories that people have to make up? The papers are bad enough, but at least they lie about things that actually happen.

I handed him the paper and sat down.

"Which section would you like to start with today?"

"The section that says we're winning the war and we don't have the food shortages any longer," I requested.

"They haven't printed that section," he said with a funny smile. He always found things so damned amusing.

"I don't really have time today," I told him. "Do you remember anything about the Grand Duke?" I asked.

"Most recently, he was going to be married to the eldest daughter of the tsar. It was, however, called off."

"Called off? Why?" I asked.

"Apparently the rumors suggest that he and the prince were up to some inappropriateness together."

"And that cost him a marriage." I was part of a larger theater now. The silk bastard wasn't just being nosy or annoying. He was on a campaign for something. I wasn't sure how, but he was more than what he seemed.

"What do you know about Rasputin?"

"The cartoons they publish about him are very entertaining. The papers claim he has the royal family under his spell, or that he's having an affair with the tsarina."

"Are they true?"

"Who knows? There are many instances of Rasputin being invited to the Summer and Winter Palaces. I've also heard rumors that he can get audiences with the tsar and have those he doesn't like sent to Siberia. There are some reproductions of letters circulating. These are correspondences between him and the tsarina. Some very tender language is used between them. 'Longing to caress your hand,' and so forth," he told me. "But there are also rumors that he is the Antichrist."

A Small Bite to Eat

I entered the hospital and climbed the stairs. I made a habit to show up earlier than scheduled and to not show myself until I was late. I wanted no surprises. Being early is almost like being a ghost. No one expects you, so no one really looks for you. If I ever needed to hide from someone, I'd just be early.

I peeked around the corner. Inside Rasputin's room, the entire hospital staff was leaning away from him like grease collecting in a tipped saucer. The two guards were still there. A man was talking to them. It was the man with darting eyes from the tavern. His hand was wrapped in cloth where I had hit it with my pipe. He cradled it very delicately.

The silk bastard's men must have looked at the hospital address the tsar gave me after they beat me. There was no other reason for him to be here. The man with darting eyes was pacing and looking at his watch. This is the second time he has been waiting for me.

I grabbed the metal pipe from my coat and slipped it into my sleeve. I swung around the corner with my right arm pressed against the wall to hold the pipe secure. When he saw me, he lifted his glove like a flag. He waved me toward him. I didn't move.

He turned his head away from me as if I wasn't worth looking at. He was irritated that I wasn't obeying. We stood for so long looking at each other that the two guards began to whisper.

When he couldn't stand still any longer, the man with darting eyes stomped down the hall, swinging his arms like he was running across a rope bridge.

"You are late," he said, spitting in my face as he spoke.

"What do you want?" I asked.

"I was asked to collect your report," he replied.

"What report?"

"I said report," he ordered, clicking his boots.

"I can hear you," I said.

I didn't know what to do. I can't do anything to him because he is my superior. I also can't even hint at the tsar's name or divulge anything about my mission on his orders. Then I saw the watch in his hand. It was my watch.

"I was told by you-know-who to gather your assessment."

I grabbed his injured hand as hard as I could and covered his mouth with his scarf again. I heard the pain go through his body.

"I don't know who you-know-who is. On the outside possibility you've been sent here unknowingly, or you're just really stupid, I'm going to pretend you weren't here and ignore you. But if you or anyone else asks me for anything after today, I will choke them to death. Now run before I put you in one of these rooms. Do you understand?"

I snatched my watch from his hand. He slowly tried to pull the scarf out of his mouth with his trembling hands.

"You better watch your back," he said as he ran.

After he left, I tucked the pipe away. I shouldn't have done that. The watch wasn't worth anything. That was really stupid.

After the man with darting eyes left, I approached the two guards.

"I'm relieving you," I told the two guards. "You can report back to headquarters. Is there anything I need to know? Anything unusual?" I asked.

"Everything with him seems to be unusual, sir," one of the guards said.

I watched the guards leave and waited. I could hear movement in Rasputin's room, but I didn't want to look through the window. I decided to wait for him out of sight down the hall.

I saw beds line the walls of the corridor. They were placed down both sides of the hall and left almost no room to walk. The nurses, wearing their dirty white uniforms, had to turn sideways to get through.

The hospital was so crowded that they couldn't put mattresses on all the beds. The sick and dying hung out of the bottom springs like fish bulging through a net. The faces were black from working in the factories, and they were thin from hunger. Rasputin must be so much better than the rest of us if he gets two mattresses while these workers are hanged by their beds.

A priest limped past the patients, covering his mouth as he prayed. He was unable to stop and give prayer to a single person; instead he was praying and chanting back and forth through the halls. The coughing, screaming, dying, praying and gargling made me feel ill, so I waited for Rasputin outside.

Rasputin emerged from the hospital like a panther that had escaped from the circus. He arched his back and rolled his neck. He rubbed his eyes so they would adjust to the outside. I followed Rasputin down the street. He was tall and walked in long, stumbling strides.

He clipped his heel on a curb and stopped suddenly, grabbing his chest in pain. He was big but not large. He seemed to have been put together by smashed together railroad ties, dirty goat hair and black satin.

He entered a tavern and sat next to the window. He spoke so softly that I couldn't hear what he ordered.

I waited in the corner. I just tried to blend into the wall.

The woman working at the tavern came toward me.

"Do you want something to eat?" she asked.

"No," I told her. "I'm waiting for him."

I surveyed the tavern to see if anyone was looking at him strangely. Everyone was looking at him strangely. They stared at him with curiosity and disgust. With so many people looking at him in such a way, it would be almost impossible to see which ones had darting eyes. I decided to stand closer to him in case something happened.

The woman brought him a plate, and he began to eat. He leaned into the table and dropped his head down like a mule. He sat in his chair like it was a saddle, pressing inward with his thighs. He slopped up his food, belching and smacking so loudly that passersby outside were searching for the source of the noise.

He shoveled in the food, rarely bothering to completely chew and not caring when bits rolled out of his moist mouth and into the thicket of his beard. He swallowed a large mouthful and immediately grabbed his chest.

He slammed his other hand on the table before grabbing the bottle of wine and gulping it down. The bottle rattled as he forced it away. He grabbed the edges of the tablecloth, grimacing and grunting. His face was strained as though he were being drawn and quartered.

"Fuck you!" he roared, his voice booming.

"Are you okay?" the tavern woman asked, touching his shoulder.

"Get away from me, you stupid cow!" Rasputin sprung from the chair and pushed her away with his arm. "You stupid fucking whores. You're all fucking whores!"

Everyone stared at him. He hunched over. After a few wet heaves and coughs, he made the sign of the cross and said, "Keep Jesus in your hearts, my children."

As he left the tavern, I stood in the middle of the room. No one took any notice of me. Everyone was looking at each other, trying to understand what had just happened. While I had seen all those actions before, I have never seen them in that order -- and so close together.

I followed him down the street, clutching my pipe. He was walking with his toes pointed inward and pushing his chest like he was trying to hold something inside his body.

Perhaps there was a reason why that woman stabbed this man. I have never seen a man survive a knife wound to the chest. I have been stabbed three times. And I was raped with a metal pipe when I was questioned. The wounds still hurt to this day. I can't imagine how painful a deep chest wound must feel.

Preparing the Watch

I followed Rasputin inside his apartment building on Gorochowaja 64. It was in a boring working-class neighborhood. The concrete building was four stories tall and had an archway over the entrance.

I stayed a few paces behind and followed as silently as I could. He was aware of me, but didn't seem to care. We entered the building.

To the right was a concrete staircase and the left was an entrance to the porter's office. Rasputin rounded the stairs to the third floor. I found the porter sanding a replacement lattice for a window.

"Can I help you, sir?" he asked, wiping his forehead. He was a short, crusty old man who blinked constantly because of his poor eyesight. More useless assets my industry collects: blind spies, mute snitches and stupid friends. The kettle on the stove began to whistle.

"What room is he in?" I asked, looking around the first floor.

"Who? And who are you, sir?" he asked. Usually, I could just show my special guard credentials. I tried to read it once, but the words were too hard to understand. This blind fool would have just as much trouble getting through the letter. Thinking about wounds and questionings gave me a headache. I took my pipe and swung it against the porter's right arm. He collapsed to the floor, knocking some pieces of lumber over.

"The money is in the lockbox under the desk!" he screamed. The kettle continued to whistle.

"Shut up. I don't want your money -- I want daily reports. Never write anything down. You will speak only to me. You will alert me immediately if you see or hear anything strange or see anybody unusual around. Do you understand?"

"Yes," he answered with tears in his eyes.

"If you don't do exactly as I say, I'll kill your entire family and cut off your eyelids that so you have to watch. Do you understand?"

"Yes," he said, crying and holding his arm in pain.
"What room is he in?"
"Apartment 20."
"Good," I said as I helped him into a chair across the room.

I prefer the right arm. I use just enough force to be painful, but not enough to cause any real damage. Now he has a reminder for the next week of the pain when he tries to do anything with his right arm. It is difficult to do anything without your right arm.

"When does he usually turn in?"
"What?" the porter asked.
"Sleep. When does he usually sleep?"
"I would say in the morning until the afternoon, but it depends," he screamed along with the kettle.

Next week, I'll have to give him another reminder. I poured water from the kettle and made the porter a cup of tea. I closed the door behind me as I left.

I walked out into the street and began to search for a secluded place where I could observe Rasputin. His building had a circular part running down the center over the archway, and it looked like a large tree trunk.

There was a small hallway that led to the building's courtyard. I walked through the narrow yellow passage and was surrounded by apartment windows staring at me.

Everything was dirty and wet. I could smell potatoes and tar. I looked up and saw Rasputin in his window. He appeared like a stain on a curtain. He closed the blinds, and I walked back into the street.

The building was in the center of the block, surrounded by similar looking apartment buildings. It was very quiet and still. This made monitoring easier.

The apartment was located between the Winter Palace and my headquarters. It was also a short distance to the Tsarskoselsky Rail Station. This apartment was just a few minutes' drive from all three spots. This is a very convenient location for a quick summons to the palace. I'm almost positive that this was the reason it was picked out for him. Rasputin must be very important indeed.

Toward the end of the afternoon, Rasputin walked to the telegram office by the rail station down the street from his apartment. He spoke to the clerk for a few moments and then left.

I followed him back to his building to be sure that he was not going elsewhere. Then I returned to the rail station and entered the telegram office. It was a well-lit, cramped room.

I approached the clerk and asked, "Did Rasputin just receive a telegram or send one?"

"I'm sorry, sir. I can't tell you that," the telegram clerk said hatefully.

I showed him my official papers, leaving my jacket open so that he could also see my pipe. His eyes opened wide, and his upper lip began to twitch. "I'm sorry, sir. He sent a telegram."

"To where?"

"To Pokrovskoe. I believe it was to an elder from his village," he said, shuffling through papers. When he found it, he pulled it up to his face and began to read frantically. "Yes, Pokrovskoe."

"Is that the message?" I asked.

"Yes, sir."

"Let me see it," I demanded. He carefully handed it over to me. I skipped down to the message.

I have secured the wood free of cost; it is to be carried away when permission to fell has been granted.

I copied down the message into my journal and dated it before I handed the paper back to the clerk.

"Keep all of his telegrams. I'll be by every few days, and I want to see every one of them," I said. He nodded his head quickly. "Don't tell anyone anything. Do you understand?"

"Yes," he said, rattling the paper in his hand.

I walked back to Rasputin's building. When the half-blind porter saw me, he flinched and moved back against the wall. I pulled him to the desk.

"Who lives in the apartments next to him?" I asked.

He quickly pulled out the register and began to fumble through the pages. His hands were trembling from the pain of his bruised arm. He pointed his shaking fingers to the names.

"How long have they been here?"

"This one for a year, and the other for almost three."

"How many?"

"This one is just one person, and the other is a family of three."

"I want you to move them to another apartment away from him. I don't want anyone on either side of him."

"Why?" he asked.

I grabbed his arm and squeezed until he recoiled. He rubbed his eyes. It was probably unnecessary to clear out the rooms next to him, especially since they had lived there for so long, but this is an assignment from the tsar himself, and I needed to be sure. The less traffic around his apartment, the safer he is.

The porter said, "I only have one other empty apartment."

"Then one of them will have to move out of the building. They have until the end of the week." I squeezed him extra hard before I let him go. He immediately grabbed his arm and pointed it away from me.

The two men whom I requested from headquarters arrived.

"Reporting as you ordered," one of them said. I knew they wouldn't ask questions and had short memories.

"Our assignment is in this building. Apartment 20. We're to watch and protect him from assassination. Eight-hour shifts. The two of you will keep watch from early morning to afternoon when he is sleeping. I want you both to report back here at one in the morning," I told them as I looked up toward the apartment.

My two men left in opposite directions. I crossed the street. The road was especially wide, but it gave me a good scouting point -- I could see almost everything. I watched the apartment for a few hours. It was quiet without much traffic. Calm places are more difficult to watch because the stillness makes your mind wander.

I heard the sound of a carriage coming toward me. It bore royal markings. It was on official business for the tsar. Had I done something? Oh no, I had busted the man with darting eyes in the hand. Twice. Did the silk bastard send guards for me?

The cab pulled up along Rasputin's apartment, and a young man jumped from the top of the carriage and went racing inside. A few moments later, he emerged with Rasputin.

Before I could cross the street, they boarded the cab and drove in the direction of the Winter Palace. I tried to follow them as fast as I could without running. Running after a royal cab would only get me shot. Soon the royal escort was out of sight. I began to run in the direction of the palace.

When I arrived at the palace, the cab by the outer gates. The driver and messenger were still on the carriage, waiting by one of the entrances.

They could not have been at the palace for more than forty minutes. After an hour, the man with white gloves escorted Rasputin back to the cab, and they departed. They sped past me in the direction of the apartment. Once they were out of sight, I began to run.

First Night on the Watch

He wouldn't leave the apartment the first night home from the hospital. He had been in his room with the shades drawn for the last few hours with no sound. It was 9:05 p.m., and the street was becoming tired. I had to pace in a circle to keep my eyes open.

I heard a faint stomping. I looked across the street and saw Rasputin exit the building. He wobbled down the walkway. He was not difficult to follow, with his large lumbering steps. I could hear the deep labored wheeze as he breathed. Each step caused him discomfort from the knife wound in his chest.

As he passed people on the street, they would either stop to stare or avoid eye contact. Either way, they usually gave him a great deal of space. Every aspect of this man brought attention -- from the large movements to the hideous odor to the shrieking profanities. I decided to stay closer when I followed him for a better reaction time.

As I drew nearer, he slowed down and turned his head to watch me. He never stopped moving forward, even with his head almost completely bent toward me. As he was looking at me, he bumped into a man and an older woman.

"I am terribly sorry," Rasputin said in his calming voice.

"Are you two alright?" he asked, straightening his priest's tunic.

"Yes, Papa," the old woman replied. "Did we hurt you?"

"No, of course not. Go with God." He made the sign of the cross with his hand, and the two travelers crossed themselves and went on their way.

Rasputin finally arrived at his destination. It was a house in a very aristocratic neighborhood. He would never be able to get in there. If I could never enter the salons of these kind of people, then he certainly couldn't. That high-class doorman will have him out on the street in under a minute. I took out my watch.

He spoke a word to the doorman and entered, making the sign of the cross again. Rasputin was inside. Not just inside, but a guest at a party. How did he do it? That was the most incredible thing I've ever seen. I couldn't help but smile.

The party was very loud. There was laughter and music. I can't imagine what a priest could be doing at an aristocratic drinking party. He would have to fend for himself with the rich. The curtains were all drawn, and I could only faintly hear bits of conversation. I stood across the street and watched the building. I wish I could get in there.

An attendant came outside and spoke with the doorman for a moment. They both looked over at me and whispered to each other. When the attendant went back inside, the doorman walked over to me.

"What are you doing here?" he asked, looking at my worn coat. "Get out of here, or I'll have the police on you." I presented him with my official papers and lit a match so that he could read it. Once he saw the official seal, he looked up at me. His eyes were so wide, they almost tipped his hat off his head. "I'm very sorry, sir. I didn't know." He ran inside and told the attendant who I was. Rasputin was good enough to drink with them, but I wasn't good enough to stand in the street.

After an hour, a window curtain was drawn back. The light flooded into the dark, damp street. I saw Rasputin studying the street with his white eyes. When he found me, his face lit up. He pointed at me and moved aside as a collection of sweating, well-dressed women looked at me with amazement and laughter. I ran.

I observed what I could of the party from down the street. How did Rasputin do it? He didn't belong in there any more than I did. It must be hot and loud in that flat. The entire party most likely had alcohol on their breath, sugar on their lips and stomachs that hung over their trousers. I was excited by the idea of a beggar like me drinking with the rich. What a thrill.

Around midnight, the party died out, and Rasputin emerged from the building. He was flanked by a man and a woman. Rasputin had his arm wrapped around the back of the woman and his face pressed up against the side of her head. The man on the other side was laughing and held Rasputin's robe in his right hand as they stumbled down the street. They advanced together like sections of a caterpillar, bumping into each other and then spreading apart.

I assumed they were making their way home until I noticed that Rasputin was leading them in the other direction. We walked for four or five blocks, turning left and right and left again. I kept my pipe close. The streets were not crowded, and the laughing and coughing echoed around the entire block. Rasputin was the most amazing person I have ever seen. Everyone was his friend. The people on the street, the aristocrats, the women. I wished I were Rasputin.

Suddenly, he stopped. He turned to look at me.

"What happened to your arm?" Rasputin asked.

"Nothing." How did he know?

"Nothing is only nothing if you're dead!" He was drunk and stammering. "Give it to me."

I held up my arm. He took out his cross and began to chant a prayer. He grabbed my numb arm and stared at me with his great wide eyes.

I felt warmth flood through me. It was as though I took a large drink of warm liquor. The painful tingling dissolved away. My arm was back to normal.

"Thank you," I said. I was dumbfounded. This man had a saintly power to heal. Is that why he was able to move about with a knife wound?

"Go with God, my son."

They turned a corner and left my line of sight. I ran to the end of the street and saw the trio of stumbling drunks enter an apartment building. It was an apartment of considerably less means than the previous one. The wood was crumbling apart, and the paint was all but worn away.

They entered a first-floor apartment. A party was developing, and faint sounds of music could be heard.

I was still excited by Rasputin. He was so charismatic and electric. I decided to follow him inside. I walked into the apartment building and toward the music and laughter. A doorman immediately stopped me.

"What are you doing here?" he asked.

"I'm here for the party."

"Liar. Get out of here."

"I came with my friend Rasputin," I said.

"Your friend? I don't think so. Get the hell out of here."

I fanned out my papers for him to see. He read them.

"I see. This is not an ordinary building. Men of rank live in this building. Some as high as a baron. Are you going to arrest someone?" He took out his papers and handed them to me.

"No." His papers were official and outranked mine.

"Then I'm afraid you will have to leave." He escorted me out by grabbing my un-numbed numb arm.

Forty-five minutes passed. This party was considerably less noisy. The window was open, and I tried to find the angle to see inside. The less I could see, the more I wanted to see.

Across the street, I found a wooden cart that was used to haul milk and cheese. I stood on top of it and used a lamppost to steady myself. The window had no curtains, and I could almost see the entire party unfold.

People moved back and forth, drinking and talking at each other. Men in clean gray tunics that went down to their thighs. Women with flowing dresses and silk ruffles and white faces. I wish I could be Rasputin.

Rasputin was surrounded by ladies with bare hands. The guests were shouting and drinking from a bottle he cradled. As he spoke, red spit would erupt from his mouth, and I could see the veins in his eyes.

When he gulped from the bottle, he would grab his chest as he swallowed. He would show his teeth in between words. He would touch the women's faces and pull down their blouses. He would grab them and grope them and lick them with his pink tongue.

Everything he did was met with laughter and cheering. After a few dances and speeches, Rasputin rested in a chair in the back of the room. He grabbed his chest and leaned into the back of the wooden chair. His hand lifted and fell along with his labored breathing.

As Rasputin sat for a few moments, I took in the dark wood and lavish comfort of the apartment. I had been inside plenty of expensive and aristocratic homes, but I had never taken any notice of them. Everything was covered in bright paint like a cake. Seeing this dirty peasant priest resting in an amber-colored chair with red cushions suddenly made me notice how clean and soft they were and how dirty and hard we were.

I shook off my thoughts and tried to focus. He was speaking to a young woman wearing a pink dress. She had the face of a doll and was blushing. Rasputin whispered into her ear. Then he silently grabbed her hand and led her into a dark closet.

After a few minutes of silence in the dark room with Rasputin, the young woman emerged in excitement, screaming and stumbling. With all of the perversion being displayed in the main room, what caused this woman to react so violently? She ran to a man in the room. Upon hearing her, the man and his friend began to chase Rasputin.

Rasputin threw a chair in front of the door and retreated down the stairs and through the back door to the courtyard. I jumped down from the cart and ran toward him, struggling to see where he was going. The two men exited through the back alley. They were screaming and grunting as they ran.

They were pursuing the priest. Rasputin stood in the driver seat of a buggy as he cracked the whip. I ran by the cab driver who was on his back against the curb, grabbing the side of his head in pain. Rasputin must have hit this driver in the head and stolen his cab. The two men who chased him soon gave up and slumped over to catch their breath.

I ran past them, trying to follow him. There were no other cabs around. He was driving out of control in the middle of the poorly lit street, laughing. He turned toward an alley. The street he was driving down only went one way and had to come out on the other side.

Once I made my way to the main road, I looked around nervously while trying to catch my breath. I heard nothing. There were no sounds of hooves or the creak of the cab. All I heard was the wind and a dog barking in the distance.

I walked back to Rasputin's apartment. It was very late, and the porter was sleeping. I quietly walked up the dirty, cold stairs and put my ear to Rasputin's door. He had not returned home yet. I waited outside in the cold.

After an hour, I could hear the echoes of laughter and the clomping of hooves. Rasputin turned the corner, driving the cab he had stolen. However, he was not alone. He had collected four other men and two women with their dresses pulled past their shoulders. He parked the cab in the middle of the road, and the passengers stepped down, laughing and coughing. They carried jugs and guitars, and their hands were as black as soot.

One man with a large ushanka stumbled back into the hind legs of the tired old horse. The animal erupted into a frenzy. It kicked, bucked and made terrible high-pitched noises. The horse lifted its leg in pain and screamed. Then Rasputin grabbed the beast by its nose and drew close to its long face. He stared into its eyes and began to chant. The horse almost immediately calmed down and stepped closer to Rasputin. It dropped its leg onto the ground and put weight on it. Finally, it lowered its face onto Rasputin's head and let out one final snort before it was totally at peace.

They trampled up to Rasputin's apartment. The gypsy with the guitar began to play as they sang, drank and danced. The noise was carried for blocks. People were lighting candles to investigate the noise as though they were searching for a ghost.

The person who was the biggest danger to Rasputin was himself. How could he drink and dance all night with no food, and all while recovering from a devastating knife wound?

A few minutes before 1:00 a.m., my two men arrived to relieve me. They had expected him to be asleep.

"He's still awake. I don't want to leave yet. You two take that cab in the middle of the road and return it," I told them.

"Return it to where?"

"It was picked up a few blocks east of here, and the cab owner had been hit in the head. If you can't find the driver, just leave it somewhere. I want it out of here."

The men climbed into the driver seat and slowly drove down the road. I watched the window for the next hour and heard no signs of fatigue from the people inside. My two men came back, and I had to send them on a few more errands before the party stopped and the gypsies with the guitars and black hands were gone.

Hours later, I heard a door open and close. It was one of the gypsy women who entered with Rasputin. When she hit the morning air, she began to shiver and covered up her shoulders. She didn't see me as she made her way down the street. Rasputin finally closed his light at six in the morning. It felt as though a storm had passed. My men returned, I was finally able to let them relieve me, and I could be done for the evening.

It was a long walk home. Was someone following me? I took the long winding way, just to be sure. I must be hearing things from being so tired. I was impressed that Rasputin could accomplish so much in one night.

I arrived at my building and struggled climbing the stairs. My body still hurt from my beating, and my arm was becoming numb again. I opened my window and sat on my bed. After almost falling asleep while walking home, I couldn't close my eyes in my own damned bed.

I pulled my coat over my ears and began to run the events of the night over and over in my head. How was he able to get into such a high-class party? He's just a peasant from Siberia, but for some reason, he had access to everyone, including the tsar.

What did he do to that girl in the closet?

If I could only turn into noise and hide with the people who live in the curtains. I can see them when the wind flips the edge out -- and they look back at you. They have his giant cat eyes that let him see in the dark like fire and black hands that play black music...

The Bathhouse

I awoke flexing every muscle. My jaw was swollen, and my arm felt dead. The window was open. I rushed to close it. I looked at my watch and was disappointed that I had only managed a few hours of sleep. I wasn't due at the apartment for another few hours but rushed out the door anyway.

When I arrived, I saw one of my men swaying at the knees. He was using the side of the building to block the icy air. I approached him and turned my back to the wind gust.

"Anything to report?" I asked.

"No. It's been quiet for hours. I don't think he's awake yet."

"I wouldn't think so," I said. After the night he had, I wouldn't be surprised if he slept for days. "I'm relieving you," I told my man.

"Yes, sir," he replied after looking at his watch. He was probably happy to be able to escape the cold. I leaned against the building and stared at the apartment. I was so tired. My eyes wouldn't stop blinking. Why was I so eager to get out of bed and stand here?

I could hear Rasputin snoring in his bed. He sounded like a sleeping bear or a dying old tree.

My eyes were jarred open by the sound of Rasputin slamming the door and exiting the building. I shook my head and followed him. I glanced at my watch. Several hours had passed. So much time had gone by, and I didn't remember sleeping.

We walked for hours up and down the street with no destination or purpose. We would walk in circles, cut through back alleys, and go up and down the same block. Rasputin spoke softly to himself. He would point and stab at the air with his fingers, only stopping to grab his chest in pain. He would breathe the sting away with wheezing gasps and profanity.

After a few hours of wandering, we approached a bathhouse down the street from his apartment. He forced the door open with his elbow and shoulder, grunting at the discomfort it caused. I looked up and down the street for anything unusual. I checked the back alley and noted the exits.

As I entered the bathhouse, I felt the warm, wet air absorb into my skin. When I inhaled, the steam would push my lungs to the sides of my body. I opened my coat to try and peel the air's wet fingers from around my throat.

I entered the warm room. Men were hanging their clothes on hooks. The walls dripped water onto the dirty white tile. Pasty white men sat on wooden benches. They spoke to each other and leaned back with their eyes closed. Small wooden buckets held the cold water that was beaten onto the men with a bushel of dried birch leaves, like someone slapping a carpet with a stick to remove the dust.

Everyone was naked, so it would be difficult to conceal a knife. I looked very strange with clothes on. I moved deeper into the bathhouse to find Rasputin.

I found the naked body of Rasputin being washed by a young man. They were in a private steam room. His limbs and head lay limp and lifeless on the wooden table. He turned onto his back to reveal his oozing black chest wound. It was leaking milky dark liquid onto his bony white chest. It ran up and down his ribs, which protruded out from his skin. The attendant tried to carefully wash the thick pus away but didn't want to get the brush too close to the wound.

Suddenly Rasputin erupted and began to slam his fist down onto the wood over and over. His lifeless body became contorted and thrashed about violently.

"Whores! Whores! Whores! Whores! Whores!" he screamed, pushing the attendant against the wall. He grabbed his chest and began to heave slowly, falling to his knees. The panicked gasping echoed against the tiles.

"Pray with me, you bastard. Pray," he instructed as he pulled the boy by the elbow down to his knees. He led the shivering boy in a prayer. The salty room became silent and still.

Then Rasputin grabbed one of the wooden buckets of cold water and threw it against the floor. The water quickly turned to steam and circled Rasputin. The steam turned into a dark cloud as it rose around Rasputin's body. He picked up the bucket and began to strike it against the ground until it finally broke into seventeen jagged pieces. He walked over to the young boy, grabbed him by the throat and threw him out of the room. Rasputin kicked pieces of the broken bucket and began to masturbate.

"Fucking whores!" he said repeatedly as he angrily masturbated. I wanted to turn away but couldn't stop watching the unnatural man with his furious contortions. When he had finished, he erupted into a coughing and spitting fit, which seemed to last for an hour. Black sludge spilled out of his purple chest like it was a punctured oilcan. Was he possessed by a demon or a marionette of the devil?

Then, as quickly as a door slamming, he stood upright and stretched his neck. He grabbed the birch twig and began to calmly slap the cool wet leaves over his oozing body.

I ran from the bathhouse. I didn't want his corruption to infect me. The damp air was making me tired, and he was sending his evil through the mist to attack me.

Rasputin was damned. I understood now why the tsar would be interested in this man. The tsar was just performing his holy duty as leader of the church to search out Satan's demons and destroy them. I expect that after he reads my report, I will be ordered to put an end to this Rasputin. I hope that I don't have to be the one to do it. I don't want to be damned.

After Rasputin emerged from the bathhouse, I followed him down the street at a distance. He would bless people as they walked by; some would stop and kiss his hand, and others would spit on him. An old couple approached Rasputin and fought over kissing his hand. I couldn't hear what they were saying, but they were very upset. They presented Rasputin with a letter and a handful of money. He took it, put it in his tunic and blessed them. They fell to their knees and kissed his hand.

As he was being exalted, Rasputin looked around with a half-smile, hoping for witnesses to this disgusting display. What could be in the letter? It was most likely a correspondence with the devil.

Rasputin walked to his apartment. I stood across the street for an hour until I saw a delivery cart approach. The deliveryman unloaded a large crate and took it inside. I quickly walked across the street in time to see the deliveryman round the stairs. I grabbed the porter and pointed to the delivery cart.

"Who is this delivery for?" I said.
"For Rasputin. It just arrived. Please don't hurt me."
"What's in it?"

"I don't know."

"Who's it from?" I asked.

"I don't know. He gets packages like this all the time!" he cried, holding his hands in front of his face.

There was shouting from upstairs. I pushed the porter away and tried to listen. All I could hear was Rasputin's wet laugh. The sound of bottles rattling was followed by more shouting. I ran upstairs to find the deliveryman holding Rasputin by the throat against the door. Rasputin was reaching for the deliveryman's crotch as he laughed. He was antagonizing the deliveryman.

"What's going on?" I asked.

"None of your business," he snarled at me as he slapped Rasputin in the face. "Apologize, you animal!" he said. He was a tall, strong-looking man with a bushy beard. I grabbed my pipe and swung it into his upper thigh. I knew it wouldn't break anything. It sent him to the floor. I used the pipe to choke him. My headache was blazing.

"Who are you?" I said into his ear as he struggled to grab the pipe.

"I just make deliveries."

"Who sent you to kill this man?"

"No one! He insulted me and tried to grab me."

I looked up to confirm his story with Rasputin, but he had opened the crate and pulled out a bottle of wine. He began drinking straight from the bottle.

"Who sends it?" I asked.

"I don't know!"

"You don't know?" I asked, pulling back on the pipe.

"He gets them from a great deal of people. I don't know -- I just make the deliveries," he screamed. I let him go.

"I'm with the police. If you tell anyone about this, I'll arrest you," I told him.

"Yes," he said, removing his hat. Then he limped away to his cart.

There were dozens of cases of wine bottles littering his entryway. He must have a small fortune in wine. Where does he get all this wine?

"Do you always get headaches?" Rasputin said.

"I don't have headaches."

"Indeed," he said as he laughed. "Allow me to help you."

"No, it's okay."

"It's the least I can do." He dropped his bottle of wine, and it poured onto the floor. He stared at me with his great wide eyes.

"Please don't," I said.
"It is already done."
The pain in my head was gone. He blinked and slammed the door.

Collecting the Post

I returned to headquarters to check in and read the board. I filled out some paperwork as poorly as I could manage. I looked around to see if there were any faces I didn't recognize or any darting eyes. Once I had a look, I climbed the stairs to the map room. All the drafters were in the exact same position as they were a few days ago. They were frozen except for slight strokes from the wrist. I approached my map man.

"You better be finished," I told him. He looked up at me and blinked rapidly.

"Yes, I'm finished." He stood up and walked to his shelf. He pulled out a roll and handed it to me. I grabbed it from him and opened it up to make sure it was correct. I also made sure the printing was readable. (Sometimes when they're in a hurry, they write street names so poorly that they can't be made out.)

I rolled the map back up and hid it away in my inner coat pocket. I nodded to the map man to let him know that he could go back to work.

"Some people have been asking about this," the map man told me. I knew what he wanted. I could have rammed that pencil through his ears, but he had me -- and he knew it. I took out some money and handed it to him.

"Do you think that will satisfy their curiosity?" I asked.

"That might do."

I walked down the stairs to see the clerk and collect any new orders or letters that may have come from my superiors. I approached his desk and stood. He never looked up to acknowledge me. He just kept scribbling on his long sheet of paper.

"Do I have anything?" I asked.

"Any what?" he responded, as though he were speaking to small child.

"Orders."

"Orders?" He closed his book and cleared all the papers and pens from his desk. Then he took out his handkerchief and rubbed it across the desk in one large gesture. "I am not your mother. I have my own responsibilities. I can't just stop whatever I'm doing at your convenience and do your job for you, can I?" he asked without moving any part of his body.

I took out some money and placed it on the table. He grabbed it and fanned it out across the clean table. After counting in his head, he closed his eyes and turned to look out the window.

I took out more and placed it on the table. He took the money and put it all inside his inner coat pocket.

"I don't have your orders. That gentleman wanted to be involved personally. He has them." Then he handed me my letters, all of which had been opened. He snapped his fingers, waved his hand and shooed me out of the room. "If you want your orders for your special assignment, you will have to see him."

"Do you have an address where I can reach him?"

"Maybe."

I slammed more money on his desk, and he looked up at me in disgust.

"You pick that up and set it down properly!" he demanded. I gathered the money and set it down as gently as I could. He passed me the address on a slip of paper. "He is expecting you."

As I walked to the silk bastard's address, I realized that special assignments from the tsar were not worth the expenses in bribes. I glanced through the different letters. The thought of walking across town to collect my papers out of my own pocket made me stomp at a furious pace. I was running the conversations with the clerk through my head, remembering every tone and sound. I could bend a metal pipe with my teeth.

I arrived at the silk bastard's home. It was freshly painted in light blue and gleamed against the concrete and brick of the rest of the street. The gate to the front door was twice as tall as anything around it and made a loud crashing sound. I knocked on the door and waited. When there was no answer, I knocked louder and harder. I was so angry that I actually dented the wood with my fist.

A stumpy, stumbling, bug-eyed little man answered the door in a servant's uniform. "There is no need to thrash the door, you peasant!" he said in a sharp whisper. "What is your business?"

I shoved the paper I was given in his face and tried to enter.

"What do you think you're doing?" He put his hand on my chest and pushed.

I instantly grabbed his hand. Luckily, I realized I shouldn't hurt him and let him go.

"Go around to the servants' entrance on the other side of the street," he instructed, closing the door in my face.

I walked around to the side of the building and the same bug-eyed servant let me in. He took me through the servants' entrance to the main reception office. I entered the silk bastard's office. It was empty.

"Wait here," he said firmly.

I looked at the large windows on either side of the room. The window facing the street looked over pale concrete and dirty pools of rainwater. The window on the opposite side looked over a lush and isolated garden. There was a bench in the middle of the garden that was never used.

The silk bastard burst into the room, followed by his servant. He sat down without acknowledging me. He picked up my papers and studied them. I could not tell if he was trying to copy the way the tsar conducted his audiences or if this was how all important and influential people received visitors.

"Do you know why you are here, my little boy?" he asked, rolling his neck around. He cocked his head to the side and looked at the ceiling.

"To collect a summons."

He jolted his eyes toward me in a silent reprimand.

"To collect a summons...sir," I said, correcting myself.

"That's better. Yes, I have your summons, but that is not why you are here. You are here so we can become friends." As he spoke to me, he slowly removed his gloves, one finger at a time. When they were both off, he put them back on, jamming the webs of his fingers together to make sure they were fit and snug.

"Now, my little boy, I know the tsar wanted to see you regarding the man called Rasputin. I just don't know what it is exactly that you are to be doing. Now I could make you tell me. But I have decided that we should be friends. I'm willing to open an exchange with you."

He pulled out the letter and placed it on the desk. "I will give you this summons if you will tell me the details of your assignment."

"I can't tell you, sir. I haven't been assigned to do anything yet. That's why I was supposed to return."

He stopped playing with his gloves and thought for a moment. I knew I had to offer something to him. I needed that summons. "I can tell you after I receive my orders."

He picked up the summons from the table. "You will come back here directly after your audience. Do you understand me, my little boy? You will, or I will have my guards after you."

"Yes, sir," I said, reaching for the summons. He pulled it away and raised his eyebrows. Even the rich demand rent. I pulled out what was left of the money in my pocket and put it softly on the table. He slid the paper across the desk, and it drifted onto the floor.

"You have to treat the summons from the tsar with the upmost respect. It is as though you are holding a piece of him. Do you understand? My little boy," he added hatefully. I grabbed it from the floor and held it carefully in my hand.

"You are excused," he said.

All truly industrious men are simple. Simple and terrible. He pretended to look at papers on his desk until I exited the room.

As I walked down the hall, the servant had his hand on my back, pushing me. He was trying to get me to walk faster. I turned around sharply, raising my hand to choke him, but stopped when I saw the summons in my hand. I lowered my head and left without further incident.

Report to the Tsar

As I left the silk bastard's home, I looked at the letter in my hand. It was torn and wrinkled in several places. The edges had folds, and there were several additional creases. Many people had obviously opened and read the summons without bothering to be discreet about it.

My summons was not until much later, and I had no money for a cab, so I decided to pass by Rasputin's apartment on my way to the palace. I couldn't stand being made to walk. Every step made me want to break the fingers of the clerk and the silk bastard. The air was cool, so I opened my coat to let it blow around me. This helped me stay focused.

When I arrived at Rasputin's building, I saw a wagon being loaded with furniture and trunks. It was the family of three moving out of the apartment next to Rasputin. I stopped and watched as the mother and her small child struggled to lift the heavy trunks.

Once the cart was loaded, the family took turns embracing the porter. They exchanged tearful goodbyes and then drove off slowly.

I buttoned my coat.

"Why did those fools embrace you? You just evicted them," I asked the porter.

"I returned their month's rent."

"Why'd you do that?"

"Because I just kicked them out of their home."

I walked back out into the street. Returning money? I would have never even considered doing that. What would be the point of returning the money? They can always find another apartment. What a fool for returning the money. He must be an idiot.

That family was foolish for living here anyway. Who does this man think he is? Does he think he's so much better than me? He must think he's some kind of saint to return the money. Some kind of fucking saint! I walked back into the apartment and beat the porter in the arm with my pipe.

After leaving him, I continued on my walk. The further I walked, the more exhausted I became and the angrier I got. I was furious with having to spend all my money bribing. And I was furious that the porter would return rent to that goddamned family, even after he kicked them out to the street. I hated that silk bastard and his silk gloves. I had to open my coat to cool down.

Someone was following me. I tried to focus. I began to backtrack and wander, hoping to lose him. I crossed the streets so often that it added an extra hour to my walk to the palace.

I was exhausted. I presented the second guard with my summons, and he passed it to a carrier who took it inside. I tried to rest against the wall while I waited, but the guard blocked me with his arm.

"Before you go in, give me all your weapons," he demanded. I handed him my pipe, my knife and my rope. I truly had no intention of trying to kill him. I should have left them at headquarters. I wonder how close I could get to the tsar with my knife. I never expected to get close to the most powerful man in the world. The guard grabbed me and checked all my pockets for weapons. He was very thorough; it seemed to take hours.

When the carrier returned, he waved me in. He stood next to me and pointed me down the hall. I didn't remember passing these halls when I met the tsar the last time. I was either being taken down another way, or they had changed the pictures and carpets since I was last here. It was like returning to a path that had become overgrown with gold and marble.

The man with the white gloves appeared on the horizon. I could see my summons in his hand.

"Follow me," he commanded.

We approached the same room that I had visited before. The man with white gloves motioned for me to enter as he remained in the hall. I felt the same heat, but the chair was gone. The man with the white gloves entered with a dirty, rotting stool brought from the servants' area. He placed the stool in the center of the room and motioned for me to sit. I was looking forward to sitting in that nice chair. When I sat on the stool, it wobbled and creaked.

The warm air and the silence wrapped their soft arms around me and made it difficult to keep my eyes open. I tried to swing my head around to stay awake. The squeaking stool was hard to keep balanced. There were six beautiful chairs placed around the walls of the room.

Finally the tsar entered, followed by his circus of pamperers and protectors. His attendants helped him sit, organize his desk and put on his reading glasses.

I handed my report to one of the attendants who gave it to another attendant. Every attendant had a turn blowing on it, rubbing it and brushing it with a rag. Finally it was put on the tsar's desk and straightened to be read. The tsar had one of his attendants put white gloves on so that he could pick up the report. My hands weren't very dirty. As the tsar, he must be very sensitive to such things.

I could only imagine how disturbed the tsar must be, reading about my observations of Rasputin. His regal and stoic face hid the shock quite well. He almost seemed indifferent. If I didn't know what was in the report, I would have thought that he was reading a boring letter.

The tsar brought the report down and folded the papers, handing them to one of his attendants.

"The report was a bit long. Next time, don't be so descriptive," he said as he stood up and left the room. He was not shocked at all. The man behind me tapped on my shoulder and walked me out of the room.

I couldn't believe he was so dismissive of all the unusual things that Rasputin had done. I was expecting an arrest order or at least outrage. I suppose Rasputin is only guilty of being disruptive and weird. The tsar most likely wants to collect a little more evidence before he passes judgment. After all, the tsar is the head of the church and will want to give his priests the benefit of the doubt before he brings his power against them.

The Cost of Doing Business

Outside the palace, I circled the block until I was sure that no one was following me. The silk bastard most likely was very anxious for me to deliver expensive information to him. I'm not giving that fop a damned thing. I wish I could snap him with my pipe. I would love to live in a world where someone like me could even touch someone like him. We longed to be like them, those people who have control over their destinies.

I arrived at the side alley of the church. The father was sweeping with a straw broom. He opened a window hatch and tossed the waste from his bucket to the alley. The black cloud made me cough and gag. He pulled up a wooden crate for me to sit on before he propped the window open with his broom.

"Why do you keep coming back here?"

"What do you know about the priest Rasputin?" I asked.

"Rasputin? The Mad Monk? The Dark One? He is no more of a priest than you are. He is a Khlysty."

"What's that?"

"A perverted religious sect. They think all sins can be purged through indulgence. But this Rasputin is nothing more than a debauched fraud. You can't do good by doing evil. If you really want to make a connection with God, come to the service and hear the word. Don't use a mystic."

"I'm not using a mystic. I'm his bodyguard. Could he be a devil?"

"A devil? Do you mean possessed by a demon or an actual devil? No. He's just a pervert."

"Are there ways of telling?"

"Yes, but an evil person like yourself wouldn't be able to see them."

"I can see evil."

"You are blinded by the corrupt men you take orders from."

"I take orders from the tsar."

"Not personally, through corruptible men."

"Personally."

"Liar."

"I swear, I have been personally ordered by the tsar to guard Rasputin." I showed him my summons. The priest was unable to speak. We listened to the hiss of the black fog.

"Is the tsar corruptible?"

"No! He is the leader of the church, the just and noble emperor."

"Then what I'm doing must be righteous."

"No, you are evil. You hurt people. That is why you get headaches."

"By order of the tsar. Then the tsar's orders are evil?"

"No!"

"So I should continue to protect Rasputin?"

"No."

"But if I don't follow his orders, I am acting against the head of the church. My headaches must be from the heat."

"You are making it confusing!" he snapped. "Now come and help me sweep." He removed the broom from the window.

"Perhaps later," I told him. I stood and handed him the crate.

I returned to my place. After I opened the window, I tried to work out Rasputin's routine. People fall into routines and spend their time in just a few places. Usually these places include their home, their work, their family and friends' homes and church. Knowing what places a person frequents can make it easier to understand them, and at the very least, follow them.

I took out the map I had drawn. Rasputin's apartment was in the center, and the streets were drawn out a few miles in every direction.

I spread out the map on the floor and flattened it with the side of my hand. I took a pin and pushed it into the map over Rasputin's apartment. After looking at my notes (and what I could remember from the things I didn't put in my notes), I placed pins in different parts of the city where Rasputin had been. I put in twenty or thirty pins before I realized that I needed a map that covered a larger area. I would have to go back to the map room.

Rasputin seems to go everywhere. I began to connect the places he had been by wrapping the red string around the tips of the pins. It quickly became cluttered and confused, and I was forced to re-tie the string three or four times. The red seemed to branch out to every edge of the map. It was like a crimson vine that crawled through parts of the city.

I left my apartment and walked with the red string burned into my mind. Rasputin was everywhere. Usually people have less than ten pins in their map. Even the most important and mobile people only have about twelve pins. He had over twenty pins.

I heard the rapid click of boots and then felt a sharp pain down my legs. I saw bright red flashes. I looked up. Two men were kicking me in the stomach and head. I tried to use my hands as a shield but the hits broke through. I saw the man with darting eyes and his wrapped hand. The silk bastard had sent these two swine after me again. I knew better than to get up and fight back. It is always easier just to stay down. I tried to fight the blackout, but couldn't keep my eyes open.

I returned to Rasputin's apartment and relieved one of my posted men. I can't remember which one I relieved, but it doesn't matter. I didn't feel like waiting.

He must be sleeping. In fact, he had been asleep all day.

A woman enter the apartment building. She was escorted by a doorman and was dressed in borrowed clothes. They were too large for her, but she did her best to make herself look proper. Her shoulders were covered is ruffled fabric, and she wore a gray veil over her white face. Her petticoat swished when she walked.

She had white teeth. Not the yellow and black, decayed teeth of the aristocrats. She was from a lower station but had clearly made something of herself. She must have arranged an appointment to meet with Rasputin. The doorman waited downstairs while the porter took her to Rasputin's room. She refused to go upstairs alone.

After some time, she emerged abruptly from upstairs. The doorman met her and she pushed him away with her arm. Her face was red, and she was trying to hold back tears. The porter's wife ran outside the office and took her in her arms.

"What happened, my dear? Are you alright?" she asked.

I had seen many women charge down the stairs in tears and fits, but this was the first time I had seen the porter's wife take them in her arms. But perhaps this was the first time I had seen the porter's wife? No, I had seen the wife before.

"I'm fine. Thank you for asking," she said, doing her best to collect herself.

"Madam, if you have just come from an audience with Rasputin, I can assure you that you are not fine," she told her.

The visitor was relieved by the porter's wife's kindness and understanding. It was as though she didn't have to pretend; they were like cousins who shared a family secret. They entered the office and shut the door.

I was able to hear the conversation because of the damage to the window that was left when I had pushed the porter into it. I crouched down to listen.

The tearful visitor wobbled slightly and used the porter's wife's arm to steady herself.

"I have seen him do very terrible things," the wife confided as she put the young woman into a chair.

"I was here on behalf of my husband," the lovely young woman began. "He is an ensign who is very sick. He is in a hospital in the city, but they're going to remove him because they don't have the space. He can't be moved -- he's so very weak.

"I had made an appointment with him to receive my petition to have my husband remain in the hospital. When I arrived at the top of the stairs, the first thing he said was, 'Come in and undress.'

"I handed him my petition, which he took. Then he said it again: 'Come in and undress.' I didn't know what to do, so I took off my clothes and followed him through the door. I can't believe I did it -- I don't know what compelled me to do so. I just did it. When I entered, he dropped the petition to the floor.

"He closed the door and began to grab me and stroke me. He fondled my face and my breasts, mumbling to himself. Then he said, 'Kiss me, kiss me... I have taken a fancy to you.' I tried to push him away as politely as possible. Then he went to his desk and wrote the note I needed for my husband. He didn't give it to me, however -- instead, he continued to touch me and push his body up against me. 'Kiss me, Kiss me... I love you,' he said, but I kept trying to push him away.

"When he tried to put his hand between my legs, I pushed him away properly. Then he put the note back on the desk and turned to me. 'I am angry with you. Come back tomorrow,' he told me. I don't understand. I was told he would help me. How can a priest use extortion?"

She grabbed the wife's hand, and the wife helped her straighten her clothes and fix her hair. What does extortion mean?

Once she was composed, she left the building. I stood up immediately.

"Excuse me, madam," I said.

She turned around and waited for my question.

"Was your appointment satisfactory?"

"I beg your pardon, but who are you?" she asked most politely.

"I'm an agent with the special police, madam." I showed her my papers, which she looked over most diligently. She might have been the first person to actually read them. Her gray veil had designs of birds in flight pressed tightly against her sad face.

"Do you know of Rasputin?" she asked.

"Yes."

"Then you know the answer to your question, sir," she said.

"Are you returning tomorrow?" I asked. I knew this was the reason I had spoken to her.

"No."

"Why not?"

"Going to him for assistance means paying money in advance, in addition to anything he cares to name. Since I cannot do that, I shall not return." She bowed her head and continued down the street, followed by the short porter.

"What does extortion mean?" I asked. She looked back at me but didn't answer. She wanted to get home while she could still maintain her composure. Her dignity made me smile and hate her.

Rasputin's Patrol

As darkness fell, Rasputin rounded the stairs and stopped to see the porter. After they spoke for a moment, Rasputin took the porter's arm in his long fingers. His black dirty claws poked and fondled his bicep. The porter winced in severe pain. Rasputin was inspecting where I had hit the porter with my pipe.

Rasputin closed his eyes and began to pray. The porter had a look of terror. Then Rasputin gazed deep into him. I could see Rasputin's alabaster eyes from across the street. He began to weep. When it was over, the porter was able to swing his arm around as though it were healed. Rasputin had healed him.

He burst through the front door of the building and marched down the street. There was a terrible smell blowing from him. It was sour and metallic, like a dead man. I wondered how the same man who could heal could also engage in sexual torments and smell like death. Rasputin wallows in this disgusting sexual deviancy. And he smiles about it. He enjoys his ugly sexuality and waits for admiration.

I had to keep following him. My legs wouldn't respond, and I was falling behind. I stopped and slapped myself in the face. I opened my coat so that the cold air would compel me.

As we wandered down the street, I found it hard to tell which street we were on. It felt as though we were passing the same apartment over and over.

Rasputin entered a lavish apartment building on the other side of town. I tried to see which apartment he was going into. I waited outside for hours, struggling to keep my eyes open and slapping myself in the face. The night was becoming colder and wetter.

Rasputin emerged with two women. It was an aristocratic lady and her servant girl. They walked the street, smiling and laughing. Then, without any warning, Rasputin grabbed the lady and began to pull down the top of her cream-colored dress that hung at her shoulders. She slapped him two or three times, but he keep grabbing the lace with his long, dirty fingers. The servant girl tried to grab him, but he grabbed her between the legs and jerked her close to his body. He pulled them into an alley between the walls of two buildings directly behind them. It was out of the way but certainly not out of sight.

He drew the servant girl toward him with his left hand while he forced the lady's dress down to her waist. There was a struggle until the lady grabbed onto the back of Rasputin's head and arched her back. There were silent screams and gasps. Crowds of gentlemen escorted their ladies past them and paid no attention.

When it was all over, Rasputin emerged, stumbling and grabbing his chest. He staggered off the side pathway and began walking down the middle of the road, blessing people as they walked by and spitting at the cabs that almost ran him over.

I ran to see if he had killed the two women but was shocked to see them emerge from the alley. Their faces were flushed, and they were struggling to pull their torn clothing over their naked bodies. I suddenly realized that I was blocking their path.

"How dare you look me in the eye! You peasant!" the lady said hatefully as she adjusted her tiny feathered hat. "Clear out of the way, or I'll sic the police on you."

I ran past them to catch up with Rasputin. But then I stopped as I suddenly became dizzy with anger. I ran back in front of the two women and pulled down their blouses, exposing their naked bodies. If Rasputin was good enough to see the bosoms of ladies of quality, then so was I. They were too startled to be quiet and too ashamed to call for help. I reached out to grab their breasts but then stopped. Their bodies were flush and dirty from Rasputin's hands. The grease and small scratches shined on their white skin. Beads of sweat were forming into ice from the cold. They ran away, fumbling with their dresses and screaming.

As I ran to catch up with Rasputin, I was both pleased and unsure about what I had just done. I had never touched a woman of that station before. She felt like any other woman. The only special thing about her was that she could replace her torn dress.

When I caught up with Rasputin, he was leaning against the wall. I could tell something had happened but did not arrive in time to see what it was. For a moment, I thought he had been attacked and began to plan how

I would escape the city. When I saw that he was fine, I calmed down. I slowly tried to regain my focus. I am usually not so easily excited.

Did I just molest two noble ladies? What is he doing to me?

I arrived at Rasputin's apartment just as he was entering the building. He grabbed the porter before he stumbled his way up to his room. The porter quickly wrote something, put on his coat and rushed out into the street.

"What are you doing?" I asked.

"Rasputin has ordered a masseuse. I'm off to fetch her."

After a short while, he returned with the masseuse. She was a small woman with a long stride. Even though I saw her face, I couldn't remember it. She made her way up the stairs and into the apartment. I turned to the porter and asked, "How often does he send for this women?"

"It depends. I'd say usually about two or three times a week," he said as he folded his scrap of paper. I made a note of it in my journal.

Two hours later, the masseuse came down the stairs.

"He wants to speak to you," she told the porter as she put on her coat.

The porter went upstairs and into the apartment. I heard a thump. The porter came downstairs with an empty case of wine. He placed the case on the street next to the other garbage. Then the porter escorted the masseuse home.

I watched the porter and the masseuse fade into the distance. I put my shoulder against the building and began to relax. I had no idea what time it was. I tried to look at my watch, but I had trouble getting my eyes to focus. I must be more tired than I thought. I remembered that I had put the watch back in my pocket but saw that it was still in my hand.

The porter was returning. He entered the building and walked into his little apartment next to his office. He shut the door and turned out his lamp. Once the building had gone to sleep, I looked down at my hand to see if my watch was still there or in my pocket. I could feel it in both places...

Watches have hands. Could my hand turn into a watch, or my watch into a hand? How many hands do we have?

I awoke flexing every muscle in my body. There was a loud banging. I was cold, so I closed up my coat. The loud bang was coming from inside the apartment building. I ran across the street and peaked through the door. I saw Rasputin standing at the porter's apartment door, banging and screaming.

"Wake up, you bastard! Wake up!" he screamed.

"What is it?" the porter demanded as he emerged from his room with a lamp in his hand. Rasputin forced his way into the room and was out of my sight.

A few moments later, Rasputin returned to his apartment, and the porter put on his coat and exited the building.

"What did he want?" I asked, still a little disoriented.

"He wants me to fetch the dressmaker from down the street," he answered reluctantly.

"At this hour?"

"If I don't try, he'll just be more upset."

The porter slowly made his way down the road. The porter's wife stuck her head around the corner. I don't think I had ever seen his wife before. I saw the wife and two small, thin children. Had they always been there? Perhaps I was just picturing them in my head. I rolled my head, trying to wake up. After a few minutes, the porter returned alone.

"Where's the dressmaker?" I asked.

"She wouldn't come." He took off his coat, leaned against the door and tried to work up the nerve to go and tell Rasputin.

After a deep breath (and a swig of something in a glass jar), up he went. I could hear shouting and banging. I couldn't tell if Rasputin was stomping his feet or attacking the porter. Either way, I was too tired to investigate. After a few moments of banging, the porter came downstairs. He put his coat back on and left the building.

"Where are you going now?" I asked.

"I am going to fetch the prostitute."

"What's going on?" I asked. "Does he send for her often?"

"Certainly more times than he sends for the masseuse."

After half an hour or so, the porter returned with the prostitute. I was standing across the street, so I couldn't see her face. When she entered the building, she found her own way to his apartment in the dark.

An hour later, she emerged, screaming and running down the stairs. Then I heard Rasputin open his door, laugh obnoxiously and slam the door. He opened the door again and began to slam it over and over again. It was frantic and angry. He laughed one last time and slammed the door for good.

The prostitute tried to get the porter to walk her home, but he had gone to bed and was not getting up to escort a woman of sin home. I walked over to her. She was so frightened that she pushed herself against the wall.

"I will escort you back," I said.

"Why?"

"It's dark. I want to make sure you get home."

"Who are you?"

"I'm police."

I held my hand out, and we walked. She was very unsure, but it was getting cold and she needed to get back. I wasn't sure if Rasputin would take this personally. When we arrived at the brothel, she thanked me and went inside. They always keep the windows shut. It makes it so hot. When I was a child, they would yell at me to keep the windows shut.

Rasputin's Personal Matters

It was morning. Rasputin was out on the streets, and I had been following him for hours. He wandered through the city, speaking to people, stopping by homes and visiting churches. He never had any specific place to be; he just picked up a scent and followed it, observing the city and seeing to his personal matters.

He made his way into the central part of the city, just outside of the business district. There was an old building with a wooden door. He walked through the door, past the reception area and directly into a cramped office. He spent almost an hour speaking with a short, fat man. I could just barely see into the window, but it appeared that they were either socializing or making some kind of arrangements. They had papers and took turns looking at them.

There were no locked doors to Rasputin. He could enter any place he wanted and sit down on the nice chairs. I looked around the street and could see people glaring at me through the corner of their eyes. They were fat businessmen and pushy salesmen who wished I would go back to my part of the city.

After the meeting was over, Rasputin left the business district and walked around in circles for hours. Suddenly a little old woman came shuffling up to him. She grabbed his hand, kissed it and forced a letter into his hand. I was too far to be able to hear them.

The woman cried, and Rasputin caressed her hand to calm her. He spoke, and she took out her purse. She presented a handful of money to him, and he swept it up into his hands. After he counted it, he took the letter from her, made the sign of the cross and sent her on her way.

She kissed his hand in gratitude and folded her hand in prayer. He crammed the letter into his tunic and continued to walk as though he had never stopped.

I followed Rasputin into a more populated area. His ears perked up as he looked across the street. There was a young woman being escorted by her grandmother. Rasputin quickly changed directions and cornered them. He grabbed the girl's coat and unbuttoned it. The grandmother tried to stop him, but Rasputin quickly threw her down. I should have crossed the street to intervene.

Rasputin struggled to push aside the young girl's hands to untie her blouse. The young lady's hair was fixed into elaborate swirls that were coming undone in the struggle. His dirty, greasy hands stained the white and blue cloth. Finally, after becoming frustrated, he began to grope the girl over the shirt while he forced his rail body onto hers. She cried out and flung her arms around. Rasputin suddenly stopped and looked at her with his penetrating eyes.

"Very good, my child. I'm proud of you. We didn't give in to temptation." He dropped to his knees, forcing the lady down as well. He grabbed her hands and said, "Let's pray."

Rasputin took out his wooden cross from around his neck and began to chant. The young lady picked up her grandmother and ran in the other direction. Rasputin continued to pray without moving.

After almost thirty minutes, I grew unsettled watching him pray. Then I heard a trampling of feet approaching. Three men with sticks were after Rasputin. I ran to intercept them, but it was too late. They tackled Rasputin to the ground as he chanted. They spit at him and tried to hit his thin body with their sticks. Even as they beat him, he continued to pray. His chanting sounded like the drone of flies around a corpse.

I took out my pipe and approached the fight. I ran my body into the biggest of the three men, which sent him to the ground. I lifted my pipe and brought it down as hard as I could onto his back. He howled with pain. I swung my pipe again. I hit one of them on the shoulder but was left open to being pummeled by the third man's body as he brought me to the ground.

I looked up and saw that while I was struggling with the third man, Rasputin had risen to his feet and was blessing us as we struggled. We fought to the sounds of this monk's chants and boots clipping against the street. As I bit the third man's ear, I was able to get on top of him.

I rose to my feet. The three men grabbed their injuries, helping each other to stand up. The crowd that had formed to watch dispersed.

Rasputin had continued walking down the street. His chants echoed through the streets and alleyways.

I returned to the post office and waited for the telegraph officer I had spoken to previously. When he returned, I pulled him aside. He instantly began to sweat and shift.

"He sent two telegrams today. The first was sent to the office in Tsarskoe-Selo. It read, 'How are you? Kisses.' The other was to Moscow, 17 Poushkinskaia. It said, 'Let me know who left on the third.'

"Let me see them," I demanded, holding out my hand.

"I don't have them. I already got rid of them."

"I told you to keep all of his correspondence."

"But I just told you what they said," he said, beginning to twitch.

"From now on, you will keep them until I have looked at them. Do you understand?"

"Yes, of course. I'm sorry."

I tapped his chest and walked toward the door. Then I thought of something.

"What does extortion mean?" I asked.

"I'm sorry?"

"Extortion. What does it mean?"

"Umm...when someone uses their position to obtain something inappropriately."

"Inappropriately? Like what?"

"Through excessive charges --"

"Isn't that everyone? Doesn't everyone use their positions like that?"

"Or through violence."

Do I use extortion? Am I like Rasputin? No, Rasputin uses extortion for money. Me...it is just my job.

The Leopard's Den

At Rasputin's apartment, I took my position across the street and watched. I heard a faint knocking and then muffled shouting. The porter ran to me.

"When you left, he had me collect the dressmaker for him. She is up there now, and they are making a lot of noise."

"More than usual?" I asked.

"Yes."

"Is she up there a lot?"

"No, certainly not as much as other women," he answered, shifting nervously.

"Are they usually this loud?"

"Everything he does is loud."

The porter returned to his office. There was a clang and then a boom. I could hear Rasputin stomping down the stairs from across the street. He said something to the porter and then kicked open the front door.

He emerged and looked at me with his large eyes. The whites were so bright that they glowed. He pulled out a chair and held out his arms as if presenting it to me. Then he walked to the bathhouse.

I walked across the street and sat down. It was an old wooden chair that was very well built. Even though the legs teetered on the uneven street, it held together without creaking. I noticed the inlay carving was faded. I ran my hands over the creases in the wood and felt an intricate floral pattern running up the back and down the side.

My attention was drawn to the knocking and banging that continued from Rasputin's apartment. I saw the porter looking up the stairs.

"I'm not sure what that noise is."

"I'll go see," I told him.

Every time I turned a corner on the stairwell, the banging became louder and more violent. I approached the door and saw that the doorknob was jerking. I grabbed it, and everything became still and silent. I put my ear to the door and could hear breathing. I tried to turn the knob, but the door had been locked.

"Let me out," someone whispered from behind the door. It was an angry but even voice. Rasputin had locked this woman in his apartment.

I went downstairs, collected the spare key and unlocked the door.

The door opened onto a small woman with rose-colored cheeks and gray eyes. She was extremely attractive. She gave me an uneasy, untrusting look.

"Where did he go?" she asked, trying to look past me.

"The bathhouse."

She took a moment to look at me. I noticed that she had a sewing kit and fabric tucked under her arm. She was the dressmaker. Rasputin must have lured her here with the prospect of a job and then locked her in.

She inched forward to test if I would try and stop her. When she saw that I was going to let her go, she ran past me, jumped down the stairs and crashed out the front door. As she fled, I could hear her tripping over the chair that Rasputin had placed outside for me.

I stood at his door for a moment, wondering what was on the other side. I wondered what the cemetery was like when the demons are away. I almost fell asleep, then my eyes jerked open, and I entered his apartment.

It was barren and bright. I expected it to be a rats' nest or a church covered in tar. There was a terrible smell that became thicker as I entered. The apartment had five rooms and was comfortable but austere. It was too nice for one monk living by himself. It was as though the apartment was trying to lie to me. It was trying to tell me that this was the home of a modest monk -- but in truth, it was something less honorable.

A crucifix hung on the wall. In front of it was a dirty area where Rasputin would kneel and pray. I could see the grime and muck where his hands and knees touched the floor. There was a large rats' hole in the corner of the room. He had taken a chair, broken off all but one of the legs and used it to plug the hole. Two Bibles were placed on top of the chair to keep it in place.

In the bedroom, the bedspread was brown and black from the filth of the occupant. The head of the bed had been propped up by another chair, and it appeared as though he slept at this crooked angle.

Soiled, slimy bandages had been thrown in a corner by the window. They were red and black and green and brown. These were used to dress his knife wound. Pieces of these disgusting bandages had been carried off into the wall by the rats. His filth seemed to not just infect the creatures but the very walls of the building as well.

I left the bedroom and saw a small table with letters stacked to the ceiling. I looked at how the letters were laid out to see if he had any particular filing system. I didn't want to look through them without knowing where they belonged. There was no organization to the letters, and all but a few of them were unopened. These were the letters that people on the street were so eager to get into his hands.

I grabbed one and carefully removed it from the envelope. The paper was wrinkled and stained from Rasputin's dirty, rough hands. The letters on the page were spinning as I tried to focus my eyes. When the letters stopped moving, I could see it was in the standard format of a petition addressed to the tsar. It was from a peasant of the government of Saratov.

I humbly beg you to consider an appeal for the remission of my son. He has been convicted to imprisonment in a fortress on account of his connection with a dissident group...

The letter went on pleading for the release of the son. I returned the letter to the envelope carefully and placed it where I found it. I picked up another one and opened it. It was an appeal for a pardon from a peasant of the government of Tambov. The writer of this letter had a brother who had been convicted for forgery of checks. I returned the letter and picked up another. A woman was begging Rasputin to lobby for the release of her uncle, a colonel who has been called up from the reserve. She attached two thousand rubles along with the letter.

Each of the letters had a payment attached to it. Rasputin was charging desperate people to put these petitions in front of the tsar. I tried to count how much money all the unopened letters represented but quickly lost track.

Extortion. Extortionist. Rasputin was taking advantage of people. He was taking advantage of desperate people. Desperation was sweet like sugar. Could he taste it, too?

I looked at my watch. Rasputin could return from the bathhouse at any minute. I replaced all the letters, locked the door and returned the key to the porter. I walked outside and set the chair back up before I crossed the street.

Rasputin returned without looking at me. He came upon the porter's wife as she was carrying some water. He began to grope and fondle her. When she tried to push him away, he began to swing wildly at her. His hand seldom made contact with the woman, and he stumbled around, struggling to stay on his feet. He was cursing and jabbing with his fingers.

The porter flew down the stairs and stood in between them. He began to scream and yell. The porter's wife was crying and scrambling to get back into her own apartment. The porter couldn't touch Rasputin because he knew I would be there in a moment to stop him. All he could do was keep his mouth shut, try to comfort his wife and hope that she would forgive him. I suddenly shut my eyes from a piercing headache.

Rasputin went up to his apartment. I was concerned with how he would react when he realized that the dressmaker was not waiting for him. I thought I heard a scream, but it was just the window being flung open. He threw his soiled bandages onto the roof of the other side of the building. It didn't seem to be enough to corrupt his own section of the building with these grotesque infestations; he needed to spread his filth to another part of the building.

It was as if Rasputin had forgotten about the dressmaker he locked in his apartment. He did not inquire about her to the porter or throw a screaming fit in his room. He just stayed silently in his room.

I felt around for my watch. Oh no! I realized I must have left it in Rasputin's apartment. I could see it in my mind. It was on his desk next to the letters. How could I have made that kind of mistake? I had created my pocket system to prevent something like this.

I had to get it back.

An Overdue Appointment

After I paid double for my post from the clerk, I noticed that I had received another secondhand summons from the eager aristocrat. That silk bastard was holding my real summons hostage, and I wouldn't get out so easily a second time.

During the entire walk to his home, I tried to construct a better lie that could get my summons and not bring the duke's anger down on me. If I betray the tsar's trust, I'm damned and dead; if I don't tell the silk bastard anything, I'm as good as dead.

I went to the map room and walked up to the man sharpening his pencil.

"I need an extension on that map I had you make for me."

"I suppose I could do that. I assume we want this just between us again." He was already counting his money.

"I need a ten-mile extension on each side."

"I assume you will want this quickly," he said, checking the sharpness of the point by bouncing his finger off the tip.

I grabbed the pencil and snapped it in half with my thumb. "I will be back in a day or two. I want these done by then. Do you understand?" I demanded as I stepped closer to him.

He didn't say anything; he just nodded his head and used his hand to cover his face.

We live in a strange time. When you feel that terrible pinch in your stomach, everything becomes simple and real.

I lifted my hand, and he shuffled back, stumbling over the desk. I handed him his pencil. He took it with his right hand. I grabbed his left hand and pulled it toward me. He sprawled out, and I pulled out my pipe. I hit him above his elbow. He screamed, and I covered his mouth with my other hand.

"Do you understand?"

"Yes," he said into my hand. I let him go and left the room, putting the pipe back under my coat.

No. I just used extortion. Rasputin is infecting me! I am becoming more like him. Like a devil. Did I always use extortion? No. It's Rasputin, not me. It must be the heat.

As I approached the silk bastard's home, I had a very strong compulsion to knock on the front door and force my way into the main entrance, but I didn't.

A servant answered the door and let me in. He constantly pushed and grabbed me, laying his clean hands on me. I could feel the heat in my chest, the type of anger that makes me nauseous and dizzy. I didn't have time to deal with this clean-smelling thing. I still hadn't imagined a lie to tell the silk bastard.

As I waited for my host to make his elaborate and rehearsed entrance, my mind went dead. I couldn't think of anything. I remembered that I was supposed to come back here after my last meeting with the tsar. All I could do was feel the room squeezing my air away. I closed my eyes and imagined what Rasputin was doing at this moment. Was he looking at the watch that I had left on his desk?

The door opened with a thunderous sound, and the two monkeys made their way to the chair behind the desk.

The silk bastard sat down and pulled out my summons for the tsar. He gripped it firmly with his gloved hand while he slammed his cane down on the desk, causing papers and folders to fall to the ground. His servant squatted down to pick up the mess but was corralled by the silk bastard's long black cane.

"If you want your summons, you have to tell me what the nature of your assignment is and the content of your conversations with the tsar," the silk bastard stated. "Keep in mind that failing to respond to a summons from the tsar is treason."

Everything that is contrary to what an aristocrat wants is always considered treason.

I couldn't think of anything to say, so I remained silent. He suddenly erupted in irritation. He stood up, grabbing his cane and forcing it into my chest. He was desperate. I could taste it like sugar. My mouth began to water.

"Look, you beggar, I'm not playing a children's game with you. You will tell me -- you have no choice. I own you."

I grabbed the cane from him and clubbed him over the head with it. He dropped onto the desk like a limp fish. He rolled onto the floor toward his servant who stood up with the papers still in his hand.

The servant bolted for the door, but I grabbed him by his coat and flung him to the ground. I punched him in the face four or five times and then used the cane to strike him on the back and arms.

Finally he began to shake, and I turned back to the silk bastard. He was rocking back and forth on the floor and crying. I stood over him and began to kick him over and over as hard as I could. I was hitting him so hard that I developed a headache.

Once I had run out of air, I sat in his chair and took deep breaths. The chair was so nice. It had a soft cushion and sturdy legs. I could really feel important in this chair.

The enjoyment was wearing off as I began to understand the implications of what I had just done. This beating was more than enough to get me executed.

I saw my summons on the table and grabbed it. I quickly left and used money I took from their pockets to pay for a cab to the palace.

I reported to the same gate. I handed my summons to the guard and allowed myself to be searched for weapons once again. The other guard took the summons and entered the palace. I was trying to rush my way in. I felt as though I would be safe if I were inside the palace.

The guard soon returned. "Your audience has been canceled."

"Why?" I asked in a panic

"It isn't your place to ask why!" the guard snapped.

"Do I need to report at another time?"

"You haven't been issued any new orders. If you are needed, another summons will be issued."

Had the news of what I had done to the silk bastard reached the palace before me? Without seeing the tsar, I won't be safe.

"The tsar must see these reports," I insisted. I knew that if Rasputin was to be dealt with, the tsar must know the full scope of his perversion.

The guard just looked at me silently, waiting for me to leave. I tried to enter the door by pushing my way in. The guards quickly grabbed me and threw me down on the ground. They began to kick me and strike me with the wooden part of their rifles. They kicked me so hard that it left an acid taste in my mouth.

"The tsar will summon you when he needs a report from you," he said forcefully.

I could see the other guard grip his rifle tighter, and I began to crawl backwards.

"You fucking whores," I said.

I left the grounds of the palace. Was the tsar turning me away because of what I did, or was he indifferent to Rasputin? It is blasphemy for the tsar to ignore Rasputin and his insanity. The tsar can't be blasphemous.

Perhaps the tsar isn't ignoring him but has made up his mind and doesn't need any more evidence. Perhaps he is working on removing Rasputin from the public. I suspect that any day now, Rasputin will be gone, and I will be reassigned.

Will I be reassigned to the front? Perhaps I will be grabbed and tied up in front of a firing squad.

I walked around, confused about where I was going, and changing my mind constantly. I found myself walking toward the old church and didn't turn around.

I went to the main door and could hear the old priest sweeping with his crooked black broom. I didn't go in but kept walking around to the side where he discards the refuse. I found the old crate and brushed it off with the backside of my hand. I sat and waited. I wanted to knock on the wood panel that covered the window. But I just sat and waited.

I wanted the priest to open the window on his own and speak to me. I wanted him to offer me help that I would refuse. After that, he would give me help anyway. But I grew impatient or frightened, so I stood up and left.

Someone Is Behind Me

Someone was behind me.

He was about ten paces behind me and wore a brown suit and hat. I couldn't make out his features. Once I caught sight of him, he rushed toward the closest door. He kept his hands in his pockets and watched me out of the side of his eye.

Was he sent to kill me? Did he have something to do with the silk bastard?

Once he saw me approaching, he ran in the other direction. I ran but was too tired to keep up. Each footstep made my headache worse and my nausea more intense.

When I stopped, I grabbed my knees and passed out. I was dizzy and confused. I had ruined my chance to grab the person who was following me. I couldn't even run a block without stumbling over. To make matters worse, I was already forgetting what he looked like. I needed to get some sleep.

I walked toward my apartment. I circled around and backtracked as much as possible now that I knew I was being followed. I turned down blind corners and crossed over side streets. It felt like it took me a day to get back home.

By the time I saw my building, I could barely keep my eyes open. My feet were so heavy that I was scraping my toes over the pavement to move forward. The black clouds of smoke coming out of the factories hovered over my apartment. The smell of burning coal and turpentine made the air dark and cold.

I entered the building and stopped at the foot of the stairs. I had to rest before I could begin my climb. How could I get up to my room without walking up the stairs? If I could become a tree, I could grow myself to the third floor and climb in the window. Did I live on the third floor or the fourth floor?

I stayed in the hall to make sure that no one waiting for me. I had been looking over my shoulder for so long that I had almost forgotten what I had done to that silk bastard. I was scared. Even though I was in a great deal of trouble, I couldn't help thinking about Rasputin.

My feet were sore, and I almost fell asleep against the wall. I entered my apartment. I hadn't been there in so long that it almost looked new. I was truly alone. I opened the window and collapsed on my bed. I put my coat over my head and closed my eyes as I waited for sleep to catch up to me. No matter how hard I tried, I could not fall asleep.

Rasputin must have been kneeling in prayer for at least a day. Maybe he was trying to pray for all of his extremely sinful behavior. And maybe he wasn't praying to God at all. Maybe that's how he controlled me.

I felt something poke me under my coat. I took out something from the inner pocket and unrolled it. It was the map extension I had ordered. I didn't remember collecting it from the map room. I didn't remember going to headquarters at all.

I quickly took an inventory of my pockets. Right front jacket pocket: official documents. Left front jacket pocket: keys and rope. Left inner jacket pocket: knife, fifteen centimeters with a black handle. Right inner jacket pocket: small leather pouch with tools for opening locks and sealed letters. Right front pants pocket: money.

I had left my damn watch in Rasputin's apartment.

I took out my money to see how much the maps cost me. I couldn't remember how much money I started out with. Did I go to headquarters in my sleep? I remember breaking the mapmaker's pencil, but I didn't remember picking the maps up.

I searched the rest of my pockets. Nothing. I reached into my back pocket and felt that my pipe was gone. Where did I leave my pipe? Had I been in a fight?

I pulled a looking glass out of my cupboard. I usually used it to look around corners and under doorways. I looked at myself to see if I had been in any fights, but I could not tell. My eyes were red and bulging as though I were being strangled. The skin on my face was rough and red as though I had been dragged across the floor. Was this evidence of a fight?

I looked down at the map that I started to build for Rasputin. I took the map extensions and pinned them to the floor so that they wouldn't slide around. Then I continued where I left off, placing pins in the different parts of the city that Rasputin travels to.

I took out the ball of red string and began to connect the points to develop some idea of his regular territory. There was no pattern, and I still needed a wider range of maps. He would travel to the quality, aristocratic parts of the city, but he would also visit poor and disgusting parts of the city.

I stepped back from the map and noticed that it looked like a red net with Rasputin's apartment at the center. It was as if he was spinning a velvet spiderweb over the entire city.

I forced myself back to bed and tried to sleep. But the minute I put my feet up, I knew that I would never be able to fall asleep. I closed the window. Then I took the pins out of the maps, folded them and put them in my coat pocket.

I went to my only chair and turned it on its side. It was old, and the wood was rotting away like dried bark. I broke off one of the legs with my boot. I would use the wooden leg until I could replace my pipe.

I took all my money from the six hiding spots I had around the room. I gathered what few things I had and rolled them up in a torn sack. I used the rope from my left front jacket pocket to fashion a strap to sling the sack across my back. I was disappointed that all that I had of value could be rolled up in a little sack. I had nothing of any true value.

I had no heirlooms, no jewelry, no watch from my father, no blankets from my mother, no rings, no suits, no silverware, no family Bible, no address book, no calendar, no deeds, no holdings, no animals, no associates, no porcelain cups for tea, no photos, no correspondence, no children, no candles, no books, no black suit, no brown suit, no watch that worked properly, no comfortable chair, no friends and no black shoes.

I had forgotten what I actually put in the sack but didn't care because I knew they weren't very important. I took one last look and then gently shut the door behind me. As I locked the door, I set a piece of the red string along the top of the door to the bottom of the frame. If someone entered, the string would break, and I'd know someone was waiting for me. I was never coming back here, but the thread would give someone the impression that I might return.

I made my way back to Rasputin's apartment and walked toward my man.

"You can go now."

"You have only been gone a few hours, sir. Are you sure you don't want to take more time?"

"Are you trying to get me to leave? Do you have something planned?" I asked

"No, sir," he said.

"Wait -- come here," I yelled.

He slowly returned. He stood with one foot pointing the other way in case he had to run. "I have an assignment for you. I want you to follow someone. He has been asking a lot of questions, and I want you to find out what you can about him."

"Yes, sir. Who is he?"

"The Grand Duke. He's that silk bastard who lives at this address." I wrote down where he lived on a slip of paper and handed it to him. "Don't draw attention to yourself."

He took the paper and disappeared around the corner.

I walked to the post office and saw the same telegraph officer. He recognized me immediately and froze.

"Has he sent or received any telegrams?" I asked.

"He hasn't received any messages, but he sent these a few days ago." He reached into a special file he kept for Rasputin and handed me a telegram. "This one was to his wife, I believe." I took it from him.

I am full of sorrow, longing to get home. A misfortune has befallen her; she will have to undergo an operation. I cannot get away. How are you? Kisses.

Then the officer handed me another message. "And this was to the same village, addressed to the head of the combined post and telegraph offices."

Give them two thousand of your own; I shall make them good in three weeks' time.

"That's it?"

"That is all right now."

I handed him back the messages and left.

A Night at the Tavern

I returned to Rasputin's building after a long, sweaty walk. The closer I got to his apartment, the more I forget about the silk bastard. I rather enjoyed myself now that I had time to think about it.

I came upon my man, who was watching the apartment carefully.

"You can go now," I told him. Did I dream about relieving him earlier, or is this the other man? How long ago did I relieve the other man?

"I just relieved you a few hours ago," he said. I had not realized that I had been watching Rasputin for so long.

"Is that a problem?" I asked.

Had both of us been watching Rasputin at the same time?

"No, sir."

"There is a dressmaker who lives down the street from here. The porter has her address. I want you to find out everything you can about her."

"Yes, sir." He crossed the street to enter the building.

I noticed that the chair Rasputin had left out for me was gone. Someone must have taken it for firewood or sold it or used it as a chair.

I tried to remember what day it was. I looked in my notebook where I kept my log of Rasputin's movements and noticed that I had stopped using dates and times when I made my entries.

I panicked at the thought of having to make up dates and times for pages and pages of entries. I had still been making entries up until I left for the palace. Was that today? It had to be today because I saw my man exit the apartment and start toward the dressmaker's home.

Was that today?

Just then, Rasputin brought out another chair. It was smaller than the one that had been stolen. He set it down in the same spot and reentered the building. Moments later, he returned with the porter.

"Right here?" I heard the porter ask. Rasputin nodded and went back inside.

The porter took the chair and nailed the back to the wood of the window frame. Confident that it was secure, he returned to his office inside.

This new chair was old and worn. Rasputin must have taken it from the porter's office. None of the legs were the same length, and a section of the seat was missing. It didn't look like it could support the weight of a small child, but Rasputin offered it to me.

The lamps on the street had been lit, and clouds covered the stars. Rasputin emerged. He scratched around his chest as he walked quickly to the other side of the street. He entered a tavern on the corner, and there was a scramble of activity, as if someone had dropped water on an anthill. Some people rushed in, and some rushed out; everyone was moving somewhere.

I followed him and sat by myself in a dark corner. He threw a large purse at the owner and ordered wine, vodka and food. He paid for drinks and songs. There were two old men who played music from their folk instruments, which they made from horses' bones and glass.

There were two fires burning at either end of the room. Long tooth-like shadows were cast on the low ceiling. It might have been the only place in the world where a priest would help you indulge in your own sin. You could see peasants, soldiers and tradesmen laughing and singing together.

A mob crowded around Rasputin. They were captivated as he yelled, spoke, snorted and sang foreign children's songs. They didn't care how offensive or frightening this monk was; they could only pay complete attention to him. It was as though he were feeding them from a bowl of pearls and silver.

I leaned against the wall. I was in this tavern with these people, but I acted invisible. Even though I had a clear mission, I had no real purpose in the tavern. I was not here to dance, drink, eat or talk. I was here to watch. I was watching a tangled puppet show that I couldn't participate in. If I did participate, I would be breaking the illusions.

An old man approached me.

"Do you want something to eat?" he asked. I had not had anything to eat in a couple of days.

"Soup," I said. I handed him some money from my right front pocket.

"That's okay, sir. He told me he would pay for your meal." Rasputin was looking directly at me. The light from the fire made his eyes burn yellow. He blessed me with his long, crooked fingers and went back to his meal. The old man slid the money back to me and went to fetch my watered-down soup.

Rasputin was very animated and excited. He pulled open his tunic to reveal a shirt and roared, "The tsarina herself embroidered this shirt for me. With her own hands, you fuckers. The tsarina! Look at the stitching. This war will tear the country apart! We all must resolve ourselves not to fight in this terrible war."

"How did she know what size to make the shirt?" yelled a sarcastic voice in the crowd.

"You don't believe me, you swine? You must all taste the honey of Jesus. Only under the bridle," he rambled incoherently. I saw those around him cheer and clap. "Behold." He produced a letter from his pocket. "A personal correspondence from the tsarina herself!" He presented the letter like a ribbon, pointing to the seal. A man came forward and inspected it.

"It's the royal seal," he said.

"Never mind the seal, you fool. You wouldn't know a seal from a cow's ass. Look at the bottom."

He leaned forward and read it.

"It says 'faithfully yours.' Then it is signed by the tsarina," he said. "What else does it say?"

Rasputin folded the letter back up and returned it to his pocket. "That is personal and not for the eyes of bastards like you." The tavern erupted into a loud roar of laughter.

I wanted to get a closer look at that letter, but I was trapped in the corner. I tried to turn away from the fire so that I didn't get too comfortable. The shrinking space and the expanding crowd made it difficult to keep my eyes straight.

The old man returned and handed me a bowl of soup. The ceramic was still hot, so I pulled my glove out of my pocket and used it to block the heat. I held the spoon with my thumb and brought the bowl to my lips. I sipped and felt the heat run through my body. This was the first meal I had enjoyed in a few days, and it tasted great. The hungrier a person is, the better their food tastes. That is why those nobles and wealthy people are so fat; they can't taste anything.

The more soup I drank, the less I could hear the loud songs and screaming from the crowd. I did feel the vibrations in my feet from the crowd's dancing on the wooden floor. It felt like a heartbeat or breathing. I took long, slow sips.

I had to lean against the wall to keep from falling asleep. It was like trying to stay awake in a slow rocking chair. I took more long sips. Then I couldn't hear anymore. I could only feel the noise as it passed through my head.

I awoke flexing every muscle in my body. The scalding soup burned my hand, and I almost dropped the bowl. Half of the people in the tavern were gone. The musicians were still playing, and someone had collected a prostitute. The men were clapping as she danced on a table. I tried to get her off the table and send her home but the men in tavern began to punch and kick me.

I tried to pull myself out of the tavern, but the heat and comfort had spread over me like ivy. I took out my knife and cut it away, pushing and stumbling. Once I was out on the street, the cold hit me in the stomach. What was I supposed to do? I widened my stance so that I wouldn't fall down.

Rasputin.

He was gone.

I ran toward his building. I beat on the porter's apartment door.

"Wake up, you bastard!"

I couldn't wait any longer and ran upstairs. I slammed into the walls as I turned up the stairs. Each step I took seemed to make four more appear at the top.

I rammed my ear into Rasputin's apartment door and held my breath. I couldn't hear any movement, and there was no lamplight shining out from the bottom of the door. For a moment, I could hear the ticking of my watch on his desk.

I had lost my assignment. I kept looking at the door. I would either have to injure myself or get out of the city. Downstairs, I was met by the porter. He looked frightened and confused.

"Did he come home yet?" I asked him.

"I don't know. I was asleep."

I walked out the door and noticed that I still had my knife out. I put it away in my jacket's left inner pocket. I'd lost him. I didn't remember falling asleep. I don't think I did fall asleep. If something happens to him tonight, I should get out of the city as quickly as possible. I could also stab myself and hope someone believes that I tried to fight them off. But they would probably shoot me just to be sure.

I looked through my maps to think of where he could have gone. But the lines and names spun and danced and became meaningless. It was too confusing to understand. Perhaps he had been collected, and I would be arrested for what I did to the silk bastard. It would be so wonderful if the tsar had ordered Rasputin to be picked up for questioning. I wouldn't have to watch him anymore or worry about his greasy hands. I was questioned once. I was hung and beaten and raped by a metal pipe. Where was my pipe? All I had now was a wooden leg.

Everything would go back to normal. But normal seemed to be just as awful.

I looked down and realized that I had sat in the chair Rasputin had left out for me. It felt so good to be off my feet that I almost fell over. My eyes were barely open, and I could smell green fog. Then a group of five or six people turned the corner and began to walk toward the building. They were all wrapped in capes and coats. Leading the group was the coughing Rasputin.

He had his arm around a woman who was laughing and reciting a children's story. Under her cape, she was completely nude. The group would laugh and snicker at different words for seemingly no reason. As the group walked past me, Rasputin stopped and blessed me with the sign of the cross. The others snorted as they filed behind him through the door. The woman continued her story, and Rasputin began to chant softly. Who were these people? I tried to widen my eyes, but they were blurry and hurt.

Rasputin tricked me. He must have known. This disgusting beast was able to outsmart me and catch me off-guard. He even has me sitting in his chair. I stood up and kicked the chair against the wall. I won't be trained like a monkey.

Rasputin opened his window and spent a few minutes spitting out of it. I could hear the laughing and singing growing louder. They played a record on the gramophone and took turns singing along. As he began to scream and laugh at the same time, his voice echoed against the cold buildings like rifle fire. The record finished its song, but they singing continued. When everyone else stopped singing, Rasputin continued. He sang with a loud and harsh voice that bounced off the walls of the street. The people around him became unsettled.

The faces that were carved into the concrete stone along the sidewalks began to blink and sneeze. I shook my head and slapped my face to wake myself up, but the stones just rolled their eyes and aimed their laughter at me. I wanted to remember how to stand up and walk into the building.

A Strange Woman

I jerked my head and saw my man standing in front of me, moving his lips. I stretched my neck. He was speaking to me.

"What did you say?" I asked.

"The clerk wants you to collect your messages and post at headquarters."

"Oh. He's sleeping. Stay here until I get back."

"There has been some trouble. Apparently a woman entered the apartment building and was asking the neighbors about him," he said.

"When?"

"I'm not sure."

"What was she asking?"

"I couldn't find that out. But Rasputin informed the police, and it was routed to us."

"You stay here," I told him. "Don't move until I relieve you."

I passed by the porter asleep in his chair, then I went up the stairs and approached Rasputin's door. I put the back of my hand to the door and felt heat. I could not tell if it was the hearth or the terrible spirits his body emanated.

How did someone get past us? It couldn't have been when I was watching.

I went to the door of his closest neighbor and knocked. When the door finally opened, I saw an old man looking at me.

"Did a young woman call on you with questions about your neighbor?" I asked.

"Yes, it was very peculiar."

"Why?"

"She wanted to know when Rasputin was here and when he wasn't. She wanted to know how much he drank, how often he had company, what kind of company."

"What did you tell her?" I asked.

"I told her nothing. I don't know any of this. Then she asked if she could sleep here."

"She wanted to sleep in your apartment?"

"Isn't that the strangest request?"

"What did she look like?" I demanded.

"She was this tall," he said, holding his hand to his chest. "She had her hair covered, and she had a round face.

"Did she have any distinct features?"

"She was confident."

"Confident? Any distinct physical features?"

"Not that I can remember," he said, rubbing his hair.

"Did she give any indication of where she was from?"

"She did keep asking how often he went to the tavern a few blocks over. I told her I had no idea about that kind of thing."

"When did this happen?"

"It was a few days ago -- I can't really remember."

I heard him close the door behind me. I was very unsettled. It was a woman who had tried to kill him before. It couldn't be the same woman because she was in prison out in the country somewhere.

The old man was right. It was very odd behavior. She was confident. While that is an unusual characteristic in this city, it is also easy to hide. How can I find someone whose only identifying feature is her confidence?

I began my walk to headquarters. My knees and ankles were tight and sore. My eyes were dry, and it hurt to blink. It felt like a long night, but I didn't remember moving at all. Or rather, I didn't remember anything.

I stood across the street from headquarters to see if anyone was waiting for me. I'm sure the silk bastard has mobilized whatever power he could by now.

I should just run, but then I would never know what would become of Rasputin.

I entered the building cautiously and looked at everyone for darting eyes. I looked in every corner and behind every door. Instead of limping, I had to walk through the pain in my joints and arm so I didn't appear weak. It was agony. Then I felt the ultimate sign of weakness: tears.

The clerk looked up at me and put down his pen.

"You haven't reported for three days," he said hatefully. Had it been that long? It couldn't have been three days.

"Are you sure?"

"Don't insult my intelligence." He pulled out a small stack of messages wrapped together in twine. I put his rent down very nicely on the table.

"Is there anything from the palace in there?" I asked.

"How should I know? Look for yourself," he said, tossing the stack on the floor. "Now get the hell out of here."

I grabbed the messages and ran out of the building. As I darted down the street, I looked through the messages for a summons or notice, discarding them onto the road as I ran.

When I was a block away from Rasputin's, I had no letters left. No summons from the palace or any word of what I did to the silk bastard. After three or four days, they had plenty of time to move on me. Are they waiting for something?

I entered the post office.

"Telegrams?" I asked.

"He received one. And sent one a few days ago. Then he just received one today."

"Let me see them."

"Here is the one he received. It is from Moscow," he said as he handed it to me.

My dear friend, we are in desperate need. He is very ill and in the worst pain. We have already allowed a priest to deliver last rights. Please help us.

I looked up at the telegraph officer.

"Then about an hour after receiving that message, he sent this one." He handed me the message.

God has seen your tears and heard your prayers. Fear not -- the child will not die.

The telegraph officer appeared to share my confused response to these messages.

"And then a day after he sent that message, he received this." He handed me the last page in his hand.

God has blessed you. He is running around and playing, free from all pain. It is as though nothing was ever wrong. You are assured a place in heaven with the angels.
Your most loyal friend.

I crumpled the page instantly. The telegraph officer and I shared a long look as we considered the series of messages.

"Where were these messages from?" I asked.

"I don't know. They were routed to avoid us knowing where it originated. But I do know that only official Imperial telegrams are routed in such a way."

Stranger Things

I relieved my man at the apartment and used the time to think. A woman went up to see Rasputin. A headache was burrowing through the front part of my brain. I had to squint my eyes and use my palm to shade them from the light. I looked far off into the distance, which brought on waves of nausea. I stared at my boots until my head stopped spinning.

The chair across the street! When I focused my eyes, I saw two young boys struggling to separate the chair from the wooden window frame. They tugged and pulled and throttled the wood. Finally they used their legs as leverage against the building.

The chair and the section of the window frame it was nailed to broke off. They gathered the wood and ran. After seeing such effort to steal a broken chair, I knew that things were going to get very, very bad.

It was late in the afternoon when an unknown woman exited Rasputin's apartment building. She had been in there for over an hour, and she tried to leave as quickly as possible. She pulled her shawl over her head and cut through the alleyway, where she most likely came to a dead end. Moments later, Rasputin emerged, tying his rope around his tunic. He yawned, grunted and went back inside.

I must sleep. I felt like I had been standing for days. My man must relieve me. Did I tell him to come right back?

Wanting will always make time bleed slowly and painfully. Rasputin had been inside for hours. No movement. He hadn't sent for anything or anyone. It was as if he were dead.

The thought of a dead Rasputin sent a pain through the left side of my head. If he were to be found dead, I could be executed on the spot. I saw my man turn the corner. Each step was slower and slower. Finally I walked toward him to halve the time.

"I'll be back in a little while. He hasn't moved. I'm going to check on him before I leave."

"I have a report for you."

"Regarding what? The confident woman?" I tried to remember what I had ordered a report about.

"The dressmaker. You asked me to find some information about her."

I had forgotten all about her. "Report then," I said.

He told me her name and address. "Anything else?" I asked.

"She lives with two other woman, all whom provide work for the store down the street."

"Where did she meet him?" I asked.

"He simply walked down the street, saw her in the store and began to follow her. He made some obscene comments and tried to undress her. She struck him in the face and has been resisting advances from him ever since."

"I see."

"Not very much information. Very straightforward. They say he does this to a lot of women. He just sends for her because she happens to live down the street." He waited for a response. "Should I continue on the dressmaker?"

"Did you check with the store?"

"Yes."

"How long has she worked there?"

"Almost seven years. Her family has lived around here for a long time."

She's no threat; she had lived here before Rasputin.

"That's all for the dressmaker. I'll be back in a little while," I repeated.

"Do you want me to send for you if he moves?" he asked.

"No," I told him directly. I had gone through extremely painful steps to keep my address away from any official source. I'm not going to give it up after the incident with the silk bastard.

I passed the porter. He nodded to me and pointed upstairs to tell me that he was still there. I climbed the stairs, walking on my toes where the sole was most worn to avoid the clicking sound.

It felt like it took me almost an hour to get from the stairs to Rasputin's front door. I forced my ear into the door. I couldn't hear any movement and could only smell the old crumbling wood. I got on my knees and placed my cheek on the dirty floor. The filth and dried mud clung to my face.

I could faintly hear him. He wasn't moving, but I could hear something. I pushed my face closer into the separation between the door and the floor. I could hear him speaking. My nose was scratching the bottom of the door. I closed my eyes and strained to listen.

He was praying. He had been kneeling for days, praying.

I exited the building and nodded to my man, who was watching the window intently. Suddenly a palace carriage from the Royal Fleet arrived. The same driver jumped out and ran upstairs. In a few moments, he emerged from the building with Rasputin. They climbed into the cab and sped away. I saw my man run after them, and I was glad I didn't have to do it this time.

I circled around to be sure no one was following me. I remembered that I wasn't to go to my apartment. How could the same man do all the terrible things and still kneel for days in reverent prayer?

I walked to the tavern a few blocks over. Why would the confident woman ask about it? I had to see about it. I couldn't sleep and needed something to keep me awake until my next shift.

I stood outside and observed. Rasputin had eaten here a few times. Why was the woman so interested in it? I looked across the street and noticed that a hotel overlooked the tavern. I decided to look inside.

The hotel was a very clean place, almost respectable. Much nicer than my apartment, but not as nice as Rasputin's. The doorman directed me to the bellboy, who directed me to the boss.

"What can I do for you?" the boss asked. I handed him my official documents. He read them over and tried to smile through his annoyance.

"I'm looking for someone," I said. "A woman."

"What does she look like?"

"I don't know. The only thing I know is that she's confident. Has a woman like that stayed here?"

"Confident?"

"Very confident." I felt like a fool repeating myself. He was preparing to dismiss me, but then he turned his head and smiled.

"Actually, now that you mention it, there is a woman who stayed here like that. A real self-assured creature. Very annoying. Not afraid of anything."

"Is she staying here now?" I asked.

"I don't think so. I don't recall seeing her as much since that Rasputin fellow stopped living here."

"Rasputin lived here?"

"Oh, yes, it was amazing. I had every room booked. He was rather destructive, though."

"Do you know what room she was in?"

"I don't recall."

"Can we check your register?"

"We don't keep a register," he said with a small grin.

"You're supposed to," I said. His grin went away. "Take me to Rasputin's old room."

I followed the boss upstairs and down the hall. He opened the room for me. It was still dirty and wrecked. There were black and yellow stains all over the wall and broken wine bottles everywhere.

"We're still cleaning up after him. But he's an amazing man," he said with reverence.

"Amazing?"

"Yes, he completely healed my arthritis pain. He rubbed his hands over it and prayed, and it has been wonderful. He's amazing."

Standing next to the boss in his room was like putting my hand into a fire. I felt a sickening burn that sizzled.

"Show me the rooms next to this one."

"Those are taken," he told me.

"Show them to me."

I grabbed him by the arm and led him out. He knocked on the door, and we heard a faint voice call, "Come in."

He opened the door. There was an old man, a woman and three children sitting around a table, folding shirts. "Is there anyone not in your family staying here?" They looked at me with frightened faces and shook their heads no.

"Show me the room on the other side," I said, closing the door.

He knocked, but there was no response. He took out his key and unlocked it. I made him enter first.

The room was clean. It was small and had only a table, four chairs and a small bureau against the wall. There were no rugs, pictures or dishes. The second room was completely empty except for a small cot.

I walked to the bureau and opened the drawer. There were pins and a single ball of yellow thread. My eyes bulged. I walked over to the table and saw small pinholes in the wood. Someone here was building the same map as me. I could see from the randomness of the holes that it had to be Rasputin. They used this table to hold the map, they put pins in the places Rasputin had been, and they strung the thread to link the points.

The confident woman was here. She kept this hotel room next to Rasputin to watch him. When he moved, she lost him. She has been searching for him.

I heard a loud yell and ran to the window. It was a very familiar sound. I looked out and saw Rasputin tripping along the street with four slight men wearing suits and tall hats and swinging canes. They stumbled violently until they reached the tavern.

The confident woman's window looked out right onto the tavern. She had been tracking him. Rasputin and his guests entered the tavern and found a table. My man arrived behind them quietly. I quickly ran out of the room and onto the street.

I entered the tavern and watched Rasputin from the corner. There were no darting eyes.

"We want wine!" he said, slamming his hand down on the table. "Do you have a gramophone?"

When Rasputin discovered that the tavern had no gramophone, he staggered on top of the table and stood. He pulled up his black satin tunic up and waved his penis around. He took out a collection of small pieces of paper and began to throw them. They floated to the ground like dead leaves.

He jumped down and walked from table to table, handing out these notes and waving his penis at patrons. It grabbed everyone's reluctant attention and silenced the room. Each paper read, "Love Freely."

After a few shrieks, Rasputin's companions were able to sit him down by offering him wine. They drank and coughed and yelled for hours.

I had just leaned against the wall when I saw Rasputin stand and begin to stumble for the door. Then I saw the confident woman. She emerged from a dark corner and hurried outside. How did I not spot her earlier? Before the door closed, I saw her look off into the distance and remove her shawl.

I immediately woke up. This confident woman was signaling something, and it was no coincidence that Rasputin was ready to walk outside. That had to be the confident woman the neighbor was talking about. How did I not see her in the tavern? She must have known how to stay unnoticed. She blended right into the ground.

Rasputin made it outside before I did, and he turned right. I had no maps of this area, so I was uncertain. I pulled out my knife, slammed my shoulder into the door and tripped outside.

The confident lady stood to block me. I stumbled over to her and grabbed her neck. If she gets to Rasputin, I'm a dead man. I knew I had to move quickly to get to Rasputin, so I used my knife and cut her face. She quickly grabbed her cheek with both hands and fell backwards, silently screaming. Now she has a feature people can remember her by. Now she can stand out. Maybe she won't be so goddamned confident.

I looked up and down the street. My man called out behind me and followed. I sprinted toward Rasputin and almost cut myself with the knife. A man stepped in front of me. He was crouched down with his arms open. I held up my knife and began to slash wildly. I felt resistance. I connected with the man's upper arm. The blade was very dull and ripped more than it sliced. He screamed and grabbed his arm, cradling it close to him.

I ran as hard as I could to catch up with Rasputin. I called to him, but he didn't take any notice of me and began to sing.

I turned and saw two men hovering over my man. They were hitting and kicking him. Then I saw two men in the distance follow Rasputin around the corner with their hands in their coat pockets. I was yelling and screaming, trying to draw attention to the street. The two men saw that I was attracting a crowd and decided not to carry out whatever they had been planning.

Rasputin suddenly stopped and looked back, finally understanding what was happening. As the two men ran away, Rasputin pulled off his boots and threw them.

"You fucking whores!" he screamed. Then he turned to me, spitting and punching the air. "What are you doing? You bastards are supposed to protect me! You fucking bastards." He began to hit and kick me until he slipped and fell on the ground. He erupted into an uncontrollable laughter that was only stopped when he grabbed his chest in pain. The putrid liquid from his wound bled through his clothes.

I walked back to my man and rolled him over. He was dead. They had stabbed him to death.

Rasputin can't be worth all this.

The Old Woman

After I was relieved, I ran directly to my young newspaper reader. Every time I saw him, he was different. Different people are annoying. He was thinner, and his clothes were more torn and haggard. I was so out of breath that I could barely speak.

"Hello. We're still losing the war," he said softly. "What are we reading today?"

"No paper. The Grand Duke."

"What about him?"

"Anything. Has anything happened to him recently?"

"I've heard he's lost great favor and privilege with the tsar. It's rumored he is to be sent to the front."

"Why? For his funny business with the prince?" I asked.

"No, I believe it's for something else, but I don't know what."

I gave him half a pencil I had in my pocket as payment and walked back to Rasputin's apartment. Being sent to the front is serious business. The tsar must consider the silk bastard an outcast to have him shipped away to war.

I was becoming more attuned to quiet noises and the yellow parts of a flame. I could hear the wind move the flap of cloth on my coat. I could feel the threading in my socks wear away. I was the tree of this street, the connection to nature and its little noises.

Through the porter's window, the sound of every door opening and closing flowed across the street toward me. I heard a slam and raised voices. I took my hands out of my pockets and walked across the street. I didn't realize how stiff I was; it took me twice as long as usual.

When I entered, I saw a little old woman screaming at the porter. He was cowering behind the desk and trying to get her to calm down. The old woman was dressed in black with a black shawl and cane. Her right arm was limp and hung dead to the side. Her face was thin and sunken from lack of food. Even though she was small and frail, her voice boomed and made my lungs vibrate.

"It's foul!" she screamed.

"What's going on?" I asked.

"Who are you?" she demanded harshly, looking me straight in the eye. Don't look at me in the eye!

I turned to the porter to get my report.

"She says the smell from his apartment is too much to bear."

"The smell is causing my grandchildren to vomit! My grandson has stopped eating!"

"What do you want me to do about it?" the porter screamed.

"Clean it! Make him leave! Do something!"

"I'll talk to him," the porter said. It was a lie.

"I'll clean it myself," she begged. "It's revolting."

The porter just stood there, trying to think of something to say.

"I'll go tell him," she said, turning to go up the stairs.

She was weak and slow. She hobbled and struggled to lift her leg. It took her almost ten minutes to climb three steps, but she wasn't stopping. I found it silly to think she would try and kill Rasputin, but it was an old woman who took a knife and plunged it into his chest.

She was dressed in mourning, so her husband had died recently. Her grandchildren were sick, and she was lame. She should be desperate. But she wasn't. I'll bet she's one of the goddamn people who are desperate but don't feel desperate. She probably even has the audacity to be happy when no one is looking! Why aren't you desperate like the rest of us?

I walked over and grabbed her. "Just go back to your home," I told her.

She turned and spat in my face.

I became so enraged that I kicked her cane, and she fell back onto the steps with a hard crash. She put her one good hand over her face. She knew what the result of standing up for herself would be.

I looked up and saw Rasputin at the top of the stairs like a long shadow. He was watching over us with one hand on his chest and the other behind his back. His eyes were open so wide that I could see their glowing white orbs screaming at me.

"Let her come and clean," he said as he descended the remaining stairs. "For the sake of her children." He helped the old woman up and handed her the cane. His voice was calming and low, like a distant thunderstorm. They made their way up the stairs. He had his arm around her, almost carrying her as he clenched his chest.

Once I was able to blink again, I walked up the stairs after them.

Even though I had no reason to be silent, I still stepped with the worn parts of my shoe to avoid making any noise. The door was open. Rasputin was standing in the corner next to his altar, watching the old woman gather dirty clothes and soiled bandages with the broken end of her cane.

She gathered everything into a small pile next to the fire. She looked at me with a strange stare. It seemed like she didn't recognize me or just assumed that everyone who kicked her looked alike.

"What do you want?" she barked at me.

"Don't worry about him, my child. He is my protector from mortal enemies," he told her.

She lit the fire and put in a small log to keep the flame alive. She used the end of her cane to fling the waste from the pile into the fire. As the waste burned, the flame turned black, and the sharp smell of disease choked the air.

I suddenly vomited in disgust -- not from the foul smell but from the willingness of the old woman to clean it. It was not enough that she cleaned, but she cleaned with the acceptance of a defeated street dog. Don't clean for him! I walked over and pushed her onto the ground. She slid into the soiled bandages, and I kicked her cane to her. Rasputin jerked to life, putting his hand on my elbow. I could feel his bony fingers clutching my arm. His long nails dug into my skin.

"Please, son, don't do this. Everything was fine."

His eyes blared and compelled me to leave. My headache was gone. I pushed my way out and down the stairs. I could hear Rasputin helping her up and handing her the cane so that she could continue cleaning.

I rushed back into the room and grabbed her again, throwing her to the floor. I snapped her cane in half over my knee and flung the pieces into the fire. Don't get up! I don't get up when I'm beaten. Don't clean for him! Why don't you spit in his face? I tried to kick her while she was down, but my foot got caught on the floor and I tripped.

Before Rasputin could get near me, I ran away. I waited in the hall for my head to stop spinning. I heard Rasputin pick her up again. He handed her a broken broom to replace her cane.

She silently burned the waste with no sign of hatred or resentment. She was thinking of her grandchildren. After so much misery, it seems like they are used to having to clean up filth. It seems we are all accustomed to cleaning up filth. Or was she hypnotized by him? Did she fall under his spell like all the others?

When I walked outside, I turned around and noticed that Rasputin had followed me. He had another chair in his hands. He put it in the same spot as the two others that were stolen. Then he blessed the chair. His long, dirty fingers cut through the air like crooked bird wings.

Once he finished with his blessing, he turned to me and motioned toward the chair. Again he was presenting it to me. The chair would be stolen, but he smiled as though he was excited to prove me wrong.

I stumbled away from my post. My eyes were blurry. I had trouble seeing if the sun was coming up or going down. Someone was waiting for me. I closed my eyes. Who was waiting? I grabbed for my pipe. My pipe was gone. I remembered I had to replace it with the wooden leg.

"I have a report for you, sir." It was my man, whom I had sent to follow the silk bastard. He was scared about his partner who had been killed.

"Report," I said, rubbing my eyes. I kept my hand on the wooden leg.

"There was nothing unusual. He seems to be preparing for a long journey, though. His home was busy with packing and moving."

"Where's he going?"

"I couldn't find that out. But I will," he reassured me. "I also discovered that he's one of Rasputin's fanatical political enemies. He's spoken privately to people in court and even in public about how dangerous he is and how he must be arrested. He has even spoken to the tsar, which ended in yelling and being sent away."

"You didn't see him speaking to any officials or emissaries?"

"No. He was just getting his house in order. I returned here because he has just gone to the palace."

My eyes bolted open. The dull headache in my head exploded to agony. He could have been going to the palace to present charges against me. But if he's packing for the front, perhaps no one will care. Especially since I guard Rasputin. Or maybe he just has nothing more to lose. He was desperate and couldn't tell anyone about what I had done. He might have been told to stay away from Rasputin. Perhaps he was not supposed to contact me at all.

"Do you know why he was going to the palace?" I asked, gripping the wooden leg tighter and tighter.

"No, but I believe he received a summons earlier in the day."

I felt better after my man said that. I let the wooden leg go and leaned against the building.

"Good work. Find out when he's going."

"Yes, sir." He turned and trotted down the street.

It was now dark. Did I fall asleep after my man left or was it dark when he was here? My confusion was beginning to panic me.

I looked across the street and noticed the porter walking down the block. I whistled and waved him over to me. I was too dizzy. He dodged an approaching horse.

"Has the old lady finished cleaning his apartment yet?"

"Yes. That was a few days ago."

"Days ago?" I asked. I became worried, and I grabbed my pipe as a force of habit. "Have I been here the whole time?" I remembered that my pipe had been replaced with a wooden leg.

"Yes, you've been standing right here. I thought you were sleeping, but I could see you moving around and talking to yourself."

That seemed almost impossible, but I began to remember things as they thawed out in my head. The screeching pain caused my eyes to blur.

"You need to get some sleep," the porter told me.

"Where are you going?" I asked.

"Rasputin has asked that I collect his masseuse for him."

"I replaced my pipe with a wooden leg."

"What?"

I grabbed him, but the pain from my head shot through my eyes. The porter handed me a card.

"What is this?" I asked.

"He told me to give this to you."

"Who?"

"Rasputin."

I took the folded paper and opened it. The letters were crooked, and the ink was smeared.

God knows you are in pain and wants to release you from it.

My headache was gone.

The Devil's Pact

My eyes twitched. I forced my attention on the street. My ears were ringing. I could hear laughing and yelping from inside the building. If this encounter happened to be a successful assassination, I would have to retreat to deep Siberia. I don't think I can catch squirrels.

My neck was fatigued, but I couldn't rest it against the building. My head could bind together with the ice, freezing and thawing until I became a part of the wall. It was still night. I would keep the cold out, the sin in, and be urinated on by drunken dogs. Suddenly there was a scream followed by a rumbling. This was a typical massage for Rasputin. Then there was a crash.

"You're a monster!" the masseuse screamed as she ran down the stairs.

"I hope you die, you ugly bitch whore!" Rasputin screamed as he chased her out into the street. His voice ricocheted off the walls. "Stupid fucking bitch whore!"

She disappeared into the dark. He limped back toward his building, laughing. He had no boots on, so he stumbled on the frozen pavement. He sat in the chair that he had left out for me. His body smoked as the heat from his skin evaporated into the frigid air. He looked out into the street, thinking. His night tunic was open, and I could see his knife wound. It had still not healed. It looked like wet slime from a dirty pond. The heat from the wound turned into vapor as it climbed up the icy air. His body had become a dark factory, with black smoke going up its stacks. Another black industry this country has produced.

The pus and black mucus oozed from the wound in his chest. He looked at me. His eyes absorbed all the light from the dying street lantern. He smelled like a dead horse, rotting from the inside out.

"You need to sleep, my son," he said to me before turning his attention back to the street. "You look terribly ill."

Suddenly a coach screeched from around the corner and stopped in front of him. The driver exchanged words with him. I couldn't hear them. It was an emissary from the palace. Rasputin had the half-sleeping porter fetch his regular tunic.

Rasputin threw the tunic over himself and tied a cord around his waist. He still had no boots, and his black and yellow feet melted the snow around him. He pulled himself up into the carriage and coughed. Then Rasputin stopped and looked at me.

"Come ride with us."

The coach rocked. I sat across from Rasputin. He prayed over a crucifix that he took from around his neck. His stiff beard moved up and down as he whispered into the cross. He reminded me of a squirrel chewing on nuts. The wooden cross had been handled so much that it looked like it had been sanded. There were dents and impressions from the owner's long yellow nails and callused fingers.

What's happening in the palace? Next to Rasputin sat a very worried emissary. But what could be more worrisome than Rasputin?

The red cushions could be seen even in the night. The padding was very firm and comfortable. The carriage drove recklessly and carelessly, especially for so late in the night. He didn't care if he hit anyone.

There was a lantern that swung with the rocking of the cab. The shadows made everyone spin. I was becoming sick from the rocking and the spinning. I closed my eyes. I was calmed by the sound of Rasputin's prayers. It was low and clear and filling, like a gulp of hot soup.

The cab pulled into the tsar's palace. Another nervous man was waiting. It was too dark for me to see which entrance we were going through. The palace guards quickly searched the coach and horses. Then the nervous man opened the cab door and stuck his head in. He shoved a lantern in my face, which irritated me. I almost ripped off his ear.

"Who is this man?" he asked.

"He is my guardian angel," Rasputin replied. I produced my official papers from my pocket and held them up next to the lantern.

"I understand." He closed the cab door and remained on the stairs of the outside coach. He knocked the top of the roof and signaled the driver to go. We rode with the nervous man hanging on the outside of the coach into the side entrance of the palace.

We were escorted through the doors and into a series of halls and open, half-empty rooms. Even in the dark of the lanterns, I could see the shimmering smooth gold marble that grew on the walls of the palace. We went deeper into the palace. I looked at Rasputin. His hands were white from grasping his cross so tightly. What would anyone in the palace want with this creature at this hour of the night?

We passed by a well-lit reception area with men gathered around a sofa, smoking and drinking. One of the men caught my eye. He was very short and wore a style that was foreign. He held his cigarette between his first and middle finger and had no facial hair. He studied me as we passed. He didn't look at me like an aristocrat; he was trying to figure me out.

The silk bastard was on the couch. He looked over at us as we passed. His eyes opened wide. Perhaps they could be beaten just like normal men. I nodded toward him and waved. I couldn't help but smile at his bruises. The foreign man caught our exchange, and his ears perked up with interest.

We were getting closer to the tsar. The rooms felt warmer. These rooms were filled with gold and smelled like frozen bread. The sound was thicker, and the air was tighter. I could see our destination ahead. A group of men were staring at a white door intently like cats outside a butcher shop. We came upon them, and then I saw the tsar himself. He turned and immediately saw Rasputin. The tsar reached out his hand and grabbed him by the arm.

"I have been praying since I was picked up, Papa," Rasputin said.

"Hurry, please!" the tsar commanded as he walked him to the door. That peasant bastard was looking directly into the tsar's eyes. No one may look into his eyes. The tsar was looking directly back, staring at his reflection in the large, wet eyes of Rasputin.

An attendant opened the door and let Rasputin in. I could see a small boy in a bed. He was white and stiff. Next to his bed was the tsarina. Rasputin entered, and the door closed behind him.

The group of men and doctors were as decorated as the palace walls. They had gold trim, frills and tassels, and they shined -- they shined and reflected all of it.

Someone whispered into the tsar's ear, and he turned around and looked at me. I couldn't tell if he recognized me or even knew that I wasn't supposed to be there. He was preoccupied with the condition of his only son. I saw something familiar on him. He was desperate. I could taste it like sugar.

I reached into my jacket's right pocket. I felt my knife. I made it all the way into the personal chambers of the tsar with a knife. How can that be? I had no intention to hurt anyone, ever. I still gripped the knife in my hand. It made me feel strong, and I was able to stand up straight. I was a lunge away from killing the most powerful man in the world, and no one knew. I guess nothing is perfect.

The door opened again, and I could see Rasputin at the foot of the bed on his knees, praying. The tsarina was also on her knees, holding her son's hand along with a cross. The attendant set down some water and left, closing the door. We stood watching the closed door for a moment. I couldn't hear anything; I could only smell the wood and alcohol.

They opened the door again, and the nurse entered with fresh towels, cloth and vinegar. Rasputin was leaning over the bed. He seemed to float above the young boy like a long, dark cloud. His eyes were open so wide that they absorbed the light and heat, like an open window in winter. He whispered to the boy as the nurse closed the door.

The door opened once more and revealed Rasputin standing and waiting. He was still clutching his cross, and his eyes were now tired and drifting.

"Papa," he said, reaching toward the tsar. "God has spared your son." He kissed the tsar's hand and stepped away from the door. When the tsar entered the room, the boy was sitting upright in his bed, holding a glass of water. He had such a large smile on his face that he could only take small sips. The sick white color had melted and cleared away to reveal a normal little boy. The nurse closed the door behind her.

The coach returned Rasputin and me to his apartment. Rasputin chanted and prayed and snorted. He was trying to fool all of us. He had fooled everyone. But I finally understood. This man wasn't a pervert or a bastard. He was a devil. Or he was a saint. The tsar must be extraordinarily desperate to turn to a man like Rasputin.

We stepped off the coach and onto the cold streets. Rasputin still had no boots and continued to pray with his eyes closed. I followed directly behind him. The sound of my boots crunching the snow sounded like ripping paper. Rasputin's whisper echoed across the buildings with the breeze. He disappeared up the stairs. Then I sat in the chair he had left for me. I was glad that no one had stolen it. And I was surprised that no one had stolen it.

I sat in his chair and watched the sun go up or down a few times. He was keeping that boy alive. The tsar's young son must have some terrible illness. It would have to be terrible for Rasputin to be the remedy. What awful thing was plaguing this young child? I can sense when someone is sick and about to die. That child should have died. He was desperate. But then Rasputin entered the room, and he was alive, better, smiling. He was smiling!

I kept trying to make sense of it. The tsar's son was dying. Rasputin entered the room and prayed, and moments later, the boy was alive and smiling. What strange and gross powers does this man have? He is keeping the young boy alive. I understood then why the tsar had such an interest in this man's safety. I understood the desperation. Rasputin was the only one who could secure the dynasty's future.

Rasputin was in command of the tsar's future. Rasputin was in command of all of our futures. This greasy degenerate held our future in his bony yellow fingers. Whatever method he possessed, it was unnatural.

Does he use the same spells on women? Did he use the same spell to keep the chair I was sitting on from being stolen? Perhaps Rasputin had cursed it. I stood up immediately and backed away until my shoulders hit the side of the building. I knew that if I sat in his chair, I would see more things that were confusing and awful.

Extortionists

I had no money for food, and I couldn't go home. But I was tired and hungry, so I decided to visit my woman. I had to bring something with me because she didn't have any food. No one had food anymore. You couldn't even steal it.

I thought about the chair that Rasputin had left out for me. He was just going to keep putting them outside for me. I might as well get some use out of them. I returned to Rasputin's apartment and spoke to my man.

"I want you to take a five-minute rest around the corner. I may not be here when you get back," I told him. He was slightly curious but didn't dare ask any questions.

I waited until I felt the street was still. I grabbed the chair and ran. I could feel Rasputin's eyes open.

Once I knew I was clear, I broke the chair into smaller pieces with my boot and gathered them into my arms. I sold it as firewood. I was able to buy more food than I had thought with Rasputin's chair. I rolled the groceries into my sack of useless possessions. I had forgot it was attached to me. I was surprised to see how empty it was.

I found my way to her apartment and beat on the door. She opened it and was very surprised to see me.

"My goodness. It has been so long since I've seen you."

I handed her the bag. She unpacked the sack while I sat down.

"Why are you giving me a glove?" she asked. She had not unrolled the sack far enough to see the food. I shook the sack like a rug, spilling everything all over the table.

She gathered the food and began to make a soup. I went to the window and opened it with the stick.

"I told you to leave this open," I yelled.

"You haven't been here in months. How was I to know you were going to be here?"

She was right. Had it really been that long? I sat under the window and let the cool breeze wash over me while she cooked.

I could smell the wonderful steam and red things dissolving in the pot. The hunger pains in my stomach reached through me. Without thinking, I stood up and grabbed the first piece of food from the table I could reach and ate it. It was bitter and hard to get down. It made the pain worse.

"Slow down -- it will be done soon," she said, trying to reassure me.

"Why do you keep this up?" I asked her.

"Keep what up?"

"Why do you let me in here?"

"Because you are such a big strong man," she said.

"Because you're desperate," I said. I could taste it like sugar. I don't know how I didn't see it before. I probably did see it before, and that's how I got in. I could always see it, and that's how I could always get in.

She put up with all this, just because I brought her food. My hunger pain shifted up to my head as I thought about what she had said. Were things so bad that we were putting up with bullies and bastards just to fucking eat? Am I just another fucking extortionist?

Two men burst into the room and sprang toward us. One of them grabbed my woman while the other jumped onto me. They had knives, so I kept one hand on his wrist and away from my body. My limbs were filled with sand and too slow. I reached into my right inner jacket pocket to grab my knife, but a sudden strike to my stomach made my arms curl inward.

I felt my back hit the wall. I lost my footing. Then I used the wall as leverage so that I could put my foot on his stomach and push off. He went tumbling across the room.

When he stood up, he ran toward me, swinging his knife. I reached behind my coat and pulled out my pipe. My pipe! Is this where I lost my pipe? I swung and clubbed his hand. I could hear the contact break his bones. He grabbed his hand and screamed. I took out my knife from my right inner jacket pocket with my free hand and quickly struck him five or six times in the stomach and side.

He fell limp. I turned to the intruder holding my woman and ran toward them. He was standing behind her, holding a knife to her throat. I should not have run toward them, but I couldn't stop. I took them both down to the ground. The impact knocked my knife out of my hand.

I got to my knees and began to hit the man with the wooden leg. I thought I had my pipe. That's right -- I replaced the pipe with a wooden leg. I brought it down with both hands. Every time I made contact with his back, the leg drove splinters into my palms. Once I saw his eyes begin to roll and wander, I bent down and put my wooden leg to his throat.

I choked him as hard as I could. I held onto the wooden leg so hard that my hands began to shake. He grabbed onto my pants and squeezed with his hands. Every strike sent painful vibrations to my joints. His nails dug into my skin, and I could feel the warm blood spill out over the skin of my thigh. I don't know if I killed him or not, but I stood up and tried to catch my breath.

I awoke flexing every muscle. They had killed her. I was sadder than I thought I would be. I searched through the room to find anything of value. I went through their pockets and took all the money. One of them had a nice watch. It actually worked. I needed a watch; I had lost mine.

I didn't go through the pockets of my woman. I wanted to be respectful, and I knew she didn't have anything anyway. That's why she let me in. The only thing she had was the meal she had cooked me. I couldn't just leave it there.

I ate the entire bowl of soup. It was essentially boiling, spiced water, but it was all my stolen chair could manage. I was breathing heavily and noticed the man's knife had sliced my hand. I went to grab a piece of cloth from my woman, then stopped and took a tie from one of the men. Even though I was no longer hungry and felt pains stretch around my body, I forced the hot soup into my mouth. The warm liquid flew down my throat, and I had to fight to keep it down.

When I finished, I stood up and felt the liquid float around in my belly. I rolled up my sack with my possessions, including the things I took from the two men, and put it over my shoulder. I looked around the room one last time and closed the door very quietly.

Once I left the building, I turned the corner of the street and saw the confident woman staring at me. She had her head covered with a wrap, but I knew it was her. She looked at me and gripped onto my shoulder. I tried to push her away but felt a pinch. When I looked down, I saw a knife sticking into me.

It was digging into my side, and my eyes became wet from the pain. She had missed my stomach because she was so short, and I pushed her and pulled away from the knife. I put my hands onto her shoulders to steady myself, then I threw her down. She hit the ground, looked up and smiled at me. The knife was still in her hand, and the blood instantly froze into ice on the blade.

She was amazing. I never saw her, and she was so natural in everything she did. I don't think anyone around even noticed she had just tried to kill me. I grabbed my hip to stop the bleeding and turned to flee. I stumbled against the wall. The pain felt like she had poured rocks into my bones.

The confident woman stood up and ran to me. She tried to stab me in the back. The tip of her blade hit the wooden leg from the chair and got stuck. It made a clicking sound. I swung around and punched her in the cheek where I had cut her. She fell back, holding the bandage. I could see the white cloth instantly turn red, like spilling wine on a tablecloth. Then I ran.

I wandered. I stopped. I used a glove to cover the knife wound in my side. I was so tired after eating, but I didn't want to fall asleep with demons and assassins after me. They must be the same people who were following me. They must be the same people who were after Rasputin. Maybe they took the cut on the confident woman's face personally.

I walked for another hour and came upon the church. I went around back and sat on my crate. I leaned my head against the brick, holding onto my stomach.

I heard a loud bang. The priest opened the window. I put my knife away and struggled to get my eyes open. He lodged the window open with the stained black broom.

"What are you doing here?" the priest asked as he poured out his pail of soot. The black smoke cloud plumed up to my chest.

"I don't know."

"Well, move on. It's dangerous to sleep in the alleys." The soot from his black beard shook off like pepper as he tried to close the window.

"Wait," I said. "I have some questions."

"Very well."

"There was a chair. It was cursed by Rasputin."

"Cursed?"

"He blessed it himself. Then I sold this chair to buy food. If I eat food that I got by trading it for something that was cursed, is the food still cursed? If I am near him, does his evil infect me and make me do evil? So that is why I get headaches."

"Evil begets evil. But I told you not to worry yourself with mysticism."

"Am I a user of extortion?"

"Yes."

"No. That is Rasputin. I just do my job."

"You use extortion and violence to benefit evil men."

"Is the tsar evil?"

"No."

"How can a man know if another man is evil?"

"When his actions and desires are in conflict with God."

"If I were evil, I would make it appear as though my actions were not in conflict with God."

"Are you evil, my son?"

"I think so," I said regretfully.

"Why?"

"I am protecting someone who is evil. I have eaten his cursed food. He makes me use extortion. I used extortion on a desperate woman."

"No, you are evil because you do terrible things. You are evil because you are violent and have no remorse. You carry a knife and use it on the weak at the benefit of terrible men and yourself."

"No. It is Rasputin. He has infected me. He uses demons to possess me. He gives me headaches."

"You had headaches before you saw Rasputin."

"No, I didn't!"

"You are evil."

I grabbed him by his beard. My hand slipped off due to the soot and dirt. There was bright silver from where I grabbed away the grime, and my hand was stained black. I used the same hand and clutched his tunic, pulling him through the window. I punched him in the face, and his nose began to bleed. I was still hot and could feel the knife's edge. I stood up, and the pain in my hip flew up and down my body.

"You can't hurt me," he said softly. He was not scared or angry or intimidated or desperate. He just bled, with his eyes tearing. He lifted his hand and blessed me. I let him go, and he fell back through the window. He slowly stood up, emptied the pail of dirt. He grabbed his broom and went back to sweeping the floor of his church.

British Intelligence

As I returned to the street, I looked at my hand and saw that it was stained black from the priest's beard. I tried to wipe the soot away onto my coat, but it wouldn't separate from my skin. I can't remember why I hit the priest, or if I even hit him at all. I couldn't tell if I was changing. I hit people all the time, but I have never hit a priest. I would never hit that priest.

I entered my tavern and stomped my boots. I saw a table of eyes dart toward me. It was the same short, foreign person whom I saw in the tsar's palace. He was still smoking his cigarettes in a peculiar way and wearing an annoying half-smile. He sat next to another foreign man who was winding his watch. They waved me over to sit with them. I nodded to the tavern owner in an obvious manner to let these foreigners think I had friends here.

As I approached their table, I saw the confident woman out of the corner of my eye. She was sitting alone, drinking tea. She still had a bandage wrapped around her cheek that went all the way around her head. She couldn't open her mouth very wide, due to the pain and the bandage. Tea with sugar and honey had provided much of her sustenance since we last met. The cloth was red from where I cut her. I don't think a woman had ever hated me as much as this woman. She was so amazing.

I limped past her and showed her my hip. When I pulled the glove away from the knife wound, blood and pus began to drip. She lifted her teacup and smiled with the good side of her face.

I sat down with the foreigner. My hip was sore and tight. I stretched out my leg to ease the pinch. We stared at each other for a long while. Long enough for him to finish a cigarette and light another one with his beautiful gold lighter. He offered me a cigarette. I nodded my head but didn't take it from him. I didn't trust that the cigarettes were harmless, so he took a deep drag before handing it to me.

When he presented the cigarette to me, I pointed at the lighter. He passed it to me, and I spent the next few minutes turning the flame on and off like a small child. I could see the dirt from my hands smudge the bright gold of the lighter.

"You look quite tired, my friend." They spoke Russian, but they had an odd timbre to their voice. I could tell they were foreign; their accents sounded like they were juggling knives.

"Don't worry about me," I told them. I looked over at the tavern owner and dusted off my shoulder. He returned the knife to his pocket and continued sweeping with his broom as though nothing happened.

"I think it's because you have been guarding him for too long. He must be doing something to you. From what we can tell, you haven't had a good night's sleep in some months now."

"Everyone needs more sleep," I told him. I tried to soften his sharp perception.

"Certainly the Grand Duke could use more sleep after what you did to him. He fabricated an interesting excuse for his excessive bruises, but it was quite transparent."

"How'd you know it was me?" I said. I enjoyed taking the credit.

"We're British -- we know everything," he said with such a condescending confidence that I almost believed him.

"Why are we here? What do you want from me?" I asked.

"Nothing. We want you to do nothing. We wait until only you are watching him. All you have to do is look the other way for a few seconds, and we'll take care of everything."

"Just have you send him to death while I'm guarding?"

"We can wound you to look as though you put up a valiant struggle."

"What's to stop you from going too far and sending me with him?"

"We have no desire to see you 'sent.' Just him."

"If he's 'sent' on the streets, I'll be in front of a firing squad the next day."

"We can smuggle you to Britain," he said. While the idea was simple and appealing, I didn't want to trust a foreigner to keep a promise, especially to a bastard like me.

"And what will keep you at your word?"

"Someone has to trust someone here," he replied. His voice was like a boot crushing snow.

"Why do you want him gone so badly?" I asked.

"I never met anyone with such an aura of evil," he answered, touching his chest.

"So the British are now worried about devils in foreign lands?"

"The British are concerned about devils anywhere," he said.

I laughed.

"We want him gone, and we are willing to pay for it." He took out his billfold and grabbed all the money he had. Then he nudged the arm of his friend, and he did the same. The British man collected all the money and handed it to me under the table.

It was more money than I had ever seen.

"Is this all?"

"No, of course not. Just think of it as a good faith payment."

"Your men can't be involved. They did try and 'send' me."

"Are you offended? You can't take that personally, my good man. If anything, you should be proud. Besides, you did cut that lovely woman's face. What was that about?"

"I was angry. And confused."

"You have to get control of yourself."

"I just don't want to trust you."

"It has to be sooner rather than later," he said. He was dealing with many small details and was having trouble keeping up with them. "Perhaps I could offer a third party to help you. Someone who has no love for Rasputin and has quite a lot to lose."

"Who?" I asked.

"The Grand Duke."

I laughed and snorted.

"He is perfect," the British man insisted. "He can arrange things you can't touch and go places you can't set foot in. All you have to do is a little dirt with your knife, and it's all just been a bitter biscuit."

"And you think that silk bastard will help me?" I asked.

"I've brought it up to him a few times, and he seems interested. Now if you could just convince him a little harder, he might be quite keen. Perhaps he could be the one to do the act, and you will not have to worry about anything," he whispered.

I was impressed at how well-thought-out the British man's plan was.

"Where should I get in touch with you?"

"Very clever. Why don't we just arrange a meeting now?" he proposed.

"If that makes you more comfortable," I agreed. "Meet me here in three days. Alone."

He lifted his head and thought for a moment. "Can we make it four?"

"Yes, before lunch. Alone," I repeated as I stood up and grabbed my gloves. "Wait a little bit before you leave here. I don't want you following me."

"Don't worry -- we'll give you plenty of time," he assured me as he searched the table for his lighter. I held up my hand and showed the British man that I had his lighter. Then I pointed to the initials carved on the side. He was not pleased to see that. Now I had something on this British man, and I could be reasonably assured that we could be in this together for the time being. He didn't think that was so damned cute as he borrowed the other man's matches to light a cigarette. You can't trust someone you don't have a little leverage with.

I put my hands in my pockets and walked outside. I walked away as though I were departing, then I quickly ducked back behind a cart that was tucked away in a dirty alley. I wanted to discover more about this British man.

He waited only a few moments before exiting the tavern. If I hadn't found the alley, he would've still been able to see me. The British man, the confident woman and the other man had a few words with each other and then departed. The confident woman went her own way while the two men continued their conversation down the street.

I followed the British man and his partner for blocks and blocks. They wore expensive clothes and took short, quick steps. My hip was throbbing, but I could still limp along close enough to follow them. I used the walls of buildings to prop me up.

Eventually, they casually removed their hats and entered a teashop. I stayed across the street as they ordered tea and cakes. Then a carriage from the tsar's palace fleet pulled up to collect the British man and his partner.

I arrived a few moments before the carriage passed through the palace gates. The British man got out of the carriage and removed his hat before entering the palace.

He was actually staying at the palace. This meant that he was not just some British citizen -- he was an official. He was an international official from the British Empire who wanted me to kill Rasputin.

He had the carriage driver drop him off at the teashop, and then he walked to my part of the city to have a meeting with me without raising any suspicion. I was relieved that he wasn't some agent sent to take care of me or test my loyalty.

I was angry that the silk bastard and I were of similar minds in regards to Rasputin. I didn't want to have anything in common with that blighter. Most people wanted Rasputin dead, and I should be happy that I wasn't shot for attacking him. Now I know he can't tell anyone about me or what I did to him. That means he couldn't tell anyone about what I might do to him in the future. That means he's still desperate.

Desperate Men

I limped back to my woman's apartment with my black-stained hands. I couldn't leave her there. I did leave her there. I needed to do something for her. I don't know why. I stepped over the broken dishes and chairs. I saw her, spread out along the floor. She was pale and still.

I panicked. The two other men I killed were gone. There was no trace of them. I got down on my knees and began to feel around. Maybe they were buried like a fox under leaves.

Nothing. They were gone.

Were they ever here? Oh God, were they ever here?

No, they had to have been here. I didn't do this on my own. Did I? I can't remember. I remember fighting, but I don't remember if I'm remembering a fight here. I remember the confident lady stabbing me. I pushed my finger into the aching knife wound. But that was later. What happened in here?

Am I the monster? Am I like Rasputin?

I grabbed my woman and lifted her stiff body. I tried to run, but the sharp pain in my side made my vision blur. I collapsed onto the floor. I was losing a lot of blood and could only move her to the bed. I put the blanket over her and closed the window for her.

I couldn't have done this. Not to her. Did I?

Help.

The priest stuck his head out of the window. His nose was swollen and bloody from where I had punched him. His beard was stained red like rust where the blood ran down. When he caught sight of me, he froze. His pail clanged against the window.

"I'm not afraid of you," he told me. He was both majestic and pathetic. He looked at me with so much disappointment that I felt my legs strain.

"I know."

"Then what do you want?"

"I have more questions," I told him. I still couldn't remove the black soot stain from my hand. I rubbed it against every surface I could find.

"Ask then," he said, setting the pail down.

"Is it possible to not remember evil?" I asked. My body was limp, but my eyes were racing. "Is it possible for a devil to make you not remember things as they happened to trick you?"

"What have you done now?"

"I don't know. I don't remember. I mean, I don't know if I did it or not." The priest studied me. "Is it possible that even the tsar can be blind to evil? That the tsar could do evil things?"

"Evil is very powerful. It can do many terrible things."

"I'm going to save the tsar."

"You are going to save him?" he laughed. "Who are you? He's the most powerful man in the world. You are a brute who beats old men."

"Why do you keep speaking to me? If I'm so evil, why do you keep helping me? You're not desperate."

"I haven't helped you. I've failed you. But you need my help more than anyone."

"Help."

"Your headaches? If you didn't need help, you wouldn't get headaches."

"It's just the heat," I said. "Rasputin doesn't get headaches."

"He is beyond my help."

"There is a man who wants to pay me to help destroy Rasputin," I said.

"If you want to fight evil, you can't take a reward for it; then you're just a mercenary. You're fighting for the payment and not for God's righteousness."

"Here, you take it," I said. I unrolled my sack, and the wind caught it like a sail. My possessions slammed into the side of the church. I took the British man's money and handed it to the priest.

"I don't want your blood money," he said calmly. "Pick it up."

I bent over and collected all of my things and rolled them back into the torn sack.

"Why do you want to do this? You are a terrible person -- why do you care if you do it for money or not? Why do you care if you do it at all or not? What difference is it to you?" he asked.

"I don't know." I couldn't think. "I just know I have to do it. And then I will do this good work. And I will do something, and it will be great. And when it's done, I won't be alone anymore."

"If you want to fight evil, then follow me," he said, opening the side door into the church. I stood up straight and began to walk toward him.

"Don't bring your weapons in here. Leave them outside."

I took off my knife and wooden leg and put them behind the door. The priest pulled me inside and pointed. "Look around," he whispered. Then he moved the broom down a couple of times and handed it to me.

I started sweeping. I worked on a small spot for several minutes. The motion didn't hurt my hip. No matter how many times I swept, I could never get through the soot to the wood floor; I just moved it around. A pile of dirt collected at my feet, and I had to fill up the soot pail and empty it in the alley where I usually sat.

"How does this get rid of Rasputin?" I asked.

After sweeping and emptying, sweeping and emptying, sweeping and emptying, I threw the broom down on the floor. A puff of black smoke surrounded it and slowly settled over the handle and straw brushes.

I stepped outside and collected my weapons from the ground. They were still warm from being in my pocket. I didn't see how sweeping would do anything for anybody. I needed to find a way to destroy Rasputin without being compensated. If I received any money, it would be just like the chair I took from Rasputin. I would be cursed and cursed and cursed. Before I could do anything great, I had to make myself right with everything else.

I found the tavern and went back inside. It was so different in the light of day. Was it even the same place? I spotted the fire and the chairs. The chairs were everywhere. It seemed to be the same place.

I walked up to the counter. I put my hand into my pocket and grabbed a handful of money. I slammed it on the table.

"Can I help you?" the tavern man asked.

"This is for a bowl of soup."

"Want anything to drink with your soup?"

"No, I'm paying for a bowl of soup."

"I don't understand."

"Someone bought me a bowl of soup; I'm paying for it." That bowl of soup was over a month ago. This might not be the same tavern. It didn't matter if it was this tavern or another tavern -- it was all the same.

"So give the money to the person who bought you the soup."

I left the money on the counter and returned to the wet streets. I was almost out of money and could not afford my next meal, not to mention a meal from months ago. Or was it weeks ago? Wait -- I had money from the British man.

I left the tavern. Rasputin was waiting for me. He threw an empty bottle at me, and I crouched down to avoid it. The glass smashed. How long had he been following me? Was he was following me, or was I following him?

He turned around and walked backwards slowly. He was stumbling from drinking too much, and he leaked black slime onto the pavement. He motioned for me to catch up with him. I limped toward him. When we were shoulder to shoulder, he began to walk again. We were like a pair of three-legged horses. He held onto my arm. He was trying to calm me or hold me back.

He smelled like vodka and wet cow. I looked into his eyes and saw tears. They collected the dirt and grime from his face and became black and gummy.

"Yes, my dear fellow, my soul is aching with sorrow; I am quite numb with grief. Sometimes I feel better for an hour or two, but it does not last. All the sorrow comes back again. It always comes back again."

"Why?" I asked.

"Because, you simpleton, the country is in a bad way," he said, holding his hand up slowly. "And because the cursed papers write about me, causing me much annoyance. I shall have to go to the law. I'm quoted hundreds of times but have never given one interview." He stopped suddenly and pushed me to face him. "You're limping. You're in pain."

"It's nothing," I said, trying to hide the pain. He looked into my eyes.

"It's alright. God doesn't want you to be in pain." He looked into me and through me. His bony fingers latched onto me like iron vines. His voice was still and distant, like an avalanche. His eyes became wider. "Release all your pain," he told me. His eyes screamed at me silently. They never blinked as they once again filled with tears. I felt warm and shivered at the same time. The street folded, and the Earth wrung itself out.

"Release."

He blinked his eyes and let me go. The pain in my hip was gone. Nothing on my body hurt. The pain was elsewhere and everywhere. I smiled, and he let me go. He continued walking, and I followed. I had no soreness or tightness. It was as if he had scooped out the wound and the discomfort. I wasn't even tired anymore.

He threw another bottle against the side of the building and lurched upstairs to his apartment. By keeping the tsar's son alive, he had forced the tsar to feed from his hand. I was not fooled. Finally I understood my shit life. I have been placed here to destroy this man. Heaven has positioned me to help in places it could not go, like a key under the door or a pistol in the rug. Could I just walk into his apartment and kill him? If I were a good man, I could.

I'm not going to be another of one of his upside-down saints or lopsided apostles. I took my fist and slammed it into my hip. The pain came swelling back, and I vomited. I sat down on the cold pavement and waited for the dizziness to settle. I was kept up all night by the throbbing pain and the nausea. I couldn't stand. I was kept down. The sky pressed its thumb down onto me, plunging me into the wet pavement. The wound had the feel of spoiled fruit. Even though my side felt like it was on fire, I kept trying to stand up.

I arrived early for my meeting with the British man at the teashop in the nicer part of the city. I stopped in an alley. I saw a stack of used wooden crates against the stone wall of the building. I grabbed a wooden crate and carried it so I appeared as if I were loading or unloading a cart. The crate also covered my torn coat, worn suit and painful limp. A limp is a sign of weakness.

I waited for hours. Had I missed the British man? Maybe he had used a different location as a cover. The wooden crate had become so heavy that I had to lean backwards to keep it from crashing onto the ground.

The moment after I set the crate down to rest my arms, the British man pulled up in his palace carriage. I quickly bent over and thrust the crate back into my chest. He climbed down with his partner. Why wasn't he alone?

He entered the teashop and waited for the carriage to drive out of sight. After a few minutes, he emerged from the shop alone and began to walk toward my part of town. I bent down to set the crate down on the ground but stopped when I realized I could sell it as firewood. It was amazing how much was just sitting around in the nicer parts of town.

I followed the British man as he made his way through increasingly dirty neighborhoods. The pain had spread from my hip to halfway up my side and down my leg. He stopped tipping his hat and began to puff more on his cigarette. He arrived at my tavern and stood outside. Now he was alone, thankfully. He didn't enter. He just stood, stiff as stone, against the building. Once the wood became heavy again, I emerged from the alley and approached him.

"What are you doing?" I asked him.

"Waiting for you."

"Why don't you wait inside?"

"Because I didn't know what would be waiting for me," he said. I would have probably done the very same thing. "What's in the crate?" he asked.

"Nothing."

"Nothing? Let me have a look inside." He didn't believe me and felt there was something suspicious. He grabbed the edge and thoroughly inspected the inside. "Why on Earth would you haul around an empty crate?"

"It's worth a lot around here," I told him.

"Ah. For firewood, I suppose."

I motioned for him to go inside.

He sat alone at a table in the corner and lit his cigarette with a match. I sat across from him. I slid my empty crate under the table.

"Unbutton your coat," I told him.

"Excuse me?" he said, raising his eyebrow.

"I want to see if you're armed."

"Won't that seem a bit ridiculous here?"

"I'd rather be ridiculous than bloody."

He snorted and raised his arms up. I pulled my chair around to his side of the table and began to search him. I ran my black soot hand along his waist and checked all of his pockets, sleeves and shoes. Spies love to become indignant over being searched. They think of their mind as their weapon. Guns and knives are for bullies, brutes and other people who look like me. I found nothing and scooted my chair back to the other side of the table.

"Was that necessary?" he asked, pointing to the black stains on his clothes from my hand.

I handed him the money back.

"I don't understand," he said.

"I can't take your money."

"I told you -- there will be more money."

"I can't take any amount of money."

"Why is that?" he asked.

"I thought you knew everything."

He smiled and rolled his head back but said nothing.

"Because evil begets evil."

"What nonsense is that?" he asked me.

"Don't worry. I'm still going to help you."

"You are?" he asked, sounding very confused.

"He must be destroyed. I don't care why you want him destroyed, but I agree with you. He is a devil who is poisoning my country." I don't know if he believed me, but I didn't care. I had a more important mission. You can't be paid to do something great; you just have to do it.

"Well, I do say, this is quite extraordinary. I'm afraid I'm at a loss for words," he said.

"I do want something from you," I said.

"Ah, here it is," he said, happy to resume negotiations.

"I have some questions."

"Questions? You mean you want information?"

"No, just some answers. What's your real interest in Rasputin? Even the British aren't that polite."

He handed me a crumpled letter, which I unfolded under the table.

"That is a reproduction of a letter from the tsarina to the tsar himself. You may read it if you like, but I will give you a brief summary. In the letter, the tsarina is persuading the tsar to appoint a Minister of the Interior. The tsar took the counsel of his wife and appointed the minister. This minister was handpicked by your man, Rasputin, and is one of the most incompetent men I have ever seen. Rasputin is using his influence with the tsarina to make decisions for the entire country. He's an evil man." He snarled his lip when he said the word "evil." He truly meant every letter of it. "He has an uncommon influence in the palace and needs to be stopped." His accent sounded like shaking a tin cup full of nails.

I didn't doubt that Rasputin had such influence; I just didn't believe the British man's motives. He didn't answer my question and most likely wouldn't. He let me keep the letter; there were many more reproductions. After he left, I traded my wooden crate for some food from the tavern.

Rasputin had control over the future of the empire in his hands. But I was the one who protected him. I had power over the man who had control. I had the future of Russia in my hands. The future of the entire world.

Stock of Provisions

I needed my questions answered. I walked back to my part of the city and found my young newspaper reader. He looked thin and starving. He shook and jerked about. If I had any food, I would have given him some. Well, I don't know if I really would have, but since I didn't have any, it was comforting to think that I would have.

"Hello," he said softly. "Are you alright? What happened to your leg?"

"Are we winning the war yet?" I asked

"I think we lost over two million soldiers; it doesn't sound like we're winning. But the good news is that the tsar has gone to the front to take command of the troops personally. Aren't we all very relieved?" he said hatefully. The tsar won't be content until he has killed every last one of his people. Then he will rule over empty cities and crowded graves.

"I have something I want you to read," I told him. I handed him the letter that the British man had just given me.

"I had to sell my glasses for food. I can't read today," he told me. He cried at the loss of his glasses. He had to sell his glasses, the thing that allowed him to read. Reading was everything to him. And now he has nothing.

"I'll read it to you." He smiled at the thought of me reading to him. I began to read the letter, and he waved his hands in the air.

"I've seen something like this before. Many of these are in circulation."

"Is it true that he appointed that minister?" I asked.

"Minister of the Interior? It appears so. I don't think that's such a rare occurrence, though. Rasputin has had many people appointed and dismissed."

"What is so special about this Minister of the Interior?"

"From what I've read, he's very anti-war and wants to bring all the troops home."

"Why would that bother a foreigner? Let's say, a British official."

"He probably wouldn't like it at all. If Russia brings all of her troops home, the Germans will have only one army to fight and one front to defend. That could swing the tide of the war against the British."

I patted the young man on the shoulder as he finished crying. I knew the British man had a motive -- I just didn't see how big it was. Of course he wants Rasputin dead. If Rasputin is keeping Russia out of the war, he has to be dealt with. And this British man has no compunction about letting my Russian brothers die so that he can save his British soldiers.

I'm not going to kill this bastard myself. I would be exposed and unprotected. I'm not going to crucify myself. But it wouldn't be illegal if members of the royal family kill him. If the royal family can destroy him, the people will be ready to trust them again, and everything will go back to the way it was.

That thought caused me sudden despair. Factory workers and broken flour jars and questionings. I was, however, looking forward to returning to the home of the silk bastard.

I pounded on the door as hard as I could. The public door, the door I was told never to enter. The irritated servant thrust the door open, prepared to yell and protest. When he saw me, his face immediately became overcast. The marks and bruises on his face still had not faded. I began to laugh uncontrollably.

He tried to close the door on me, but I caught the frame with my boot. I almost couldn't overpower the servant pushing on the other side because I was short of breath from laughing. It felt so good to see him in his nice pressed suit with cuts and bruises all over his face. I didn't even notice the pain down my side. He stumbled back and fell over a chair. I laughed so hard that I had to gasp for air. I rested my head on the door.

"I'm not going to hurt you, you fool," I said as I picked him up. "Where is he?"

"Upstairs."

"Let's find him together," I told him. His eyes curved at the thought of someone as low as me going upstairs, into the private chambers of an aristocrat. I pulled him close to me and put my arm around him. No one could walk in front of anyone else anymore. We would roll into each other.

The servant pulled me around like a sled dog. I found myself giggling like a little girl. I had come upon the silk bastard's palm trees. There were ten of them in five staggered rows of two. These plants only grow in the center of the world. I grabbed one of the palm fans and pulled. The entire trunk bent toward me, bowing to me. It was a tough and pointy plant. I took out my knife and cut off the branch.

The servant took me to the private drawing room of the silk bastard. I closed the door, pushing the servant into the hall. I saw the silk bastard stand.

"What is this nonsense?" he said indignantly. I held the palm fan in my hand. I touched my cheeks with my hand. I had made them sore by smiling so much. "What are you doing with that?" he asked.

"Just making myself at home," I said.

"Who on Earth do you think you are speaking to me like that?"

"I'm your new best friend," I said.

He became enraged. "How dare you, you beggar."

"I've heard the last 'beggar' from you," I told him, shoving the palm into his face. He fell backwards onto the couch. He wanted to protest but quickly remembered the beating I gave him.

I had heard the last "beggar" I was ever going to hear from anyone.

"I am here because we want the same thing. The end of Rasputin," I told him.

"I don't know what you're talking about."

"Maybe you need a moment to think about it." I was about to strike him, but I stopped when I saw the green branch in my hand. I thought it was my pipe. It was so green and pointed. He seemed confused.

"To get this done, we need each other. After it's all over, we'll never have to see each other again. Maybe you'll be married to the tsar's daughter. Think about it. That's what you wanted all along. Now I'm just giving you a way to do it."

"Let us consider that I went along with your proposal. What would your plan be?"

"What was your plan?"

"I had no such plan."

"You had no plan?" I asked, shocked and a little irritated. I don't know why I was surprised. It made sense that he would find a solution where he really didn't have to do anything.

"I was going to have him exposed and exiled."

"I'm afraid we're beyond that. We need something more radical."

"Very well. How do you suggest I participate?" he asked.

"You will be doing the killing," I told him.

"I can't kill him. I have a reputation to protect. I'm the damned tsar's nephew. I mean, the tsar's damned nephew."

"Yes, you are his nephew, so it is your duty to relieve him of this nightmare. It is your duty to your family and your country."

"You have my permission to assassinate him," he said as if speaking to one of his servants. I laughed at his simple nature.

"That won't do."

"You have my permission."

"And if I'm caught, I can expect you to speak up for me?"

"You have my word of honor."

"It won't do."

"I'm a member of the royal family, you beggar."

I slapped him in the mouth with an open hand. He leaned back and became very still.

"I can't trust a person who has such a reputation to protect. Especially the tsar's damned nephew. You will do it, and you can regain your popularity with the working people and the peasants," I told him.

"The people love me," he said with no hesitation. I had no doubt he never stopped believing that. Nobles always refer to the people as though they were one person. As though they could walk up to this people-person and demand. I was a people-person, and I wanted to cut his throat and go out into the city and kill everyone who looked like him.

"I will need to recruit some confederates to assist us."

"No. I don't want people knowing about this."

"I would only involve people I trust completely."

"Who?"

"It is none of your concern." I stared at him without blinking. He tried to look away. I wasn't going to let him organize the entire business and then leave me to the firing squad.

"Oh, very well," he relented. "The prince."

"The prince? That cross-dressing drug addict?"

"He is the most beautiful man I have ever known," he said, bolting out of his chair. He stepped closer as if to challenge me. I poked him with the palm. He continued, "He's perfect. He has just the reputation that won't be bothered by further scandal. And I think he will be willing -- he endures a unique hatred for him."

"Why?"

"That is not your concern. How should the deed be done? Shooting, stabbing, hanging?"

"Someone already tried to stab him, and that didn't work."

"Then how?" he asked.

"How do nobles normally kill people?"

"Poison?"

"Precisely"

"Very well. I know a doctor who can supply us with the poison."

"How many people do you plan on involving in this?" I asked.

"We need support."

"As you please. We should do this as soon as possible," I told him.

He rang his bell, and the servant came in.

"When is the next evening I will have available?" he asked. The servant reached into the desk and pulled out a leather-bound book. He flipped through the pages while the silk bastard put on his gloves. The servant showed him the book, "I can't possibly fit it in until after December 16."

"That's months away," I said.

"I am the Grand Duke; I can't just clear my social calendar."

I left the room and took the palm branch with me. The servant led me to the door. I didn't have to rush out. I didn't have to worry about being at anyone's mercy. I found a nice plush chair to sit in and leaned back. I looked around to take it all in. I coughed black smoke and tried to clean my soot hand.

"What are you doing?" the servant asked.

"Resting my feet for a moment," I said, not looking at him. I had to get off my feet to relieve the pain. He shuffled around me like a barking dog trying to get me out of the chair. I opened my eyes and looked at him.

"What is the matter with you?" I said. He didn't know how to respond. "I have black soot on my hand and can't get it off."

"I'm sorry?"

"I know you have to serve the Grand Duke diligently, but is it really such a bother for me to sit here a few minutes?" As he pondered that, I came to the conclusion that it wasn't a bother at all. "What do you have to eat?" I asked.

I forced the servant to take me to the kitchen. It was bustling with activity.

"Prepare a meal for this man," he told one of the cooks. I was given soup, bread and duck. It was very filling and tasted better than any food I have ever had. It was spiced and sweet. The meat and bread were warm, not soft and slimy. I could feel the sugar and salt dancing in my body. It was a perfectly straight line. Not one curve.

"All of you eat like this every day?" I asked. They looked at each other with blank stares. I saw the door to the pantry. I walked in and was filled with uncontrollable rage. The silk bastard's pantry was a palace of food and spices. I pulled the cabinets down and crushed the jars with my boot.

I grabbed salt, sugar, flour, potatoes and spices. I tried to get as much into my torn sack as possible. My hand was still stained with soot.

"What are you doing?" the servant said.

"Why can't I get the black soot off my hand?"

"You can't take that," he said, coming toward me.

"Why is that?" I said, standing up with the heavy sack on my back. It was a small fortune. I handed him the palm tree branch. As I left the kitchen, I grabbed one more slice of bread and bent forward to meet the hard light of the outside world.

At the front door, I saw a cane rack with the very cane I beat the silk bastard with. I picked it up and used it to walk. It made the pain a little more manageable when I stepped. I looked weak with a cane. I looked weak. I was weak.

Once I returned to my part of the city, I tried to sell or trade what I had taken from the silk bastard's pantry. I had trouble finding someone with anything to trade. No one had yeast to mix with the flour to make bread, no one had tea to sweeten with sugar, and no one had any meat to flavor with spices. I couldn't trade for money, and if I could, no one would have any food for me to purchase. I might as well been carrying stones around on my back.

I tried to wipe the black soot stain away.

When I arrived at Rasputin's apartment, I walked up to the porter. He thought I was going to hit him again. I took off my sack and unrolled some food for him. I gave him flour and sugar.

I took another handful of food and knocked at the door of the one-armed old lady with my boot. She answered and spit in my face. I would have slapped her, but my hands were full. I shoved the food into the arm of the old woman. She threw it back at me and slammed the door in my face. Sugar and flour hit the ground and billowed into a white cloud. It combined with the blood on my coat and formed a gum. I was about to leave, but I remembered breaking her cane. I left the silk bastard's cane against her door and limped across the street.

I watched Rasputin's apartment. He had hibernated over the past few days. He only went to the bathhouse and only called people in to visit him.

I saw my man approach and moved my knife into my hand. Who was he really? He approached slowly.

"We have some troubling news," he said. I gripped my knife tighter.

"I have heard, from several people, that Rasputin is due to be assassinated."

"By who?" I asked.

"By the prince."

"The prince? That sounds ridiculous."

"I've heard it from several people."

"Credible?"

"Both credible and not credible. They said it was going to happen in December."

"Did they say anything else?" I asked.

"No. What do we do?"

"There is nothing we can do," I said, trying to calm him. "There is always talk about Rasputin and assassination. We just keep doing our job." He seemed slightly upset. "Go get some sleep," I told him.

"You look like you could use some sleep, too."

"I can't sleep while Rasputin is alive," I screamed. After my man left, I waited and waited. I kept a sharp eye on the corners and streets. The streets wobbled with the wind. Does Rasputin control the wind? I was not worried for Rasputin but for myself.

Banging. Slamming. Rasputin's bony hands against the porter's door. The porter. I whistled. He crossed the street toward me.

"He wants me to fetch the damned dressmaker," he said, half asleep. I couldn't really understand him; it was like hearing a conversation through a windowpane.

"How many times for this poor woman?" I asked.

"Until he's satisfied," the porter said.

Rasputin harassed this woman hundreds of times. He could never have enough. He has a hole in his soul. I realized that we all have holes. But his emptiness ran up and down his body. He was not really a man but a sewer pipe.

Footsteps. The porter was walking with a woman. Was it the dressmaker or some other woman? They entered the building, and I walked into the porter's office.

"Dressmaker?" I asked.

"Yes," he said shaking his head in confusion.

"Why?" I asked.

"I don't know."

I waited all night. Before morning, she cautiously opened the door and crept out. She was no longer a poor victim but a baptized follower. How did he turn these women into initiates with his terrible lusts? She covered her head with her shawl and looked out of the side of her eyes to see if anyone was watching her.

When she saw me, she froze. I had seen many unknown and covered women leave his apartment early in the morning. The image of this woman leaving was different because I knew who she was. I knew her name and where she lived. It's different when you know them. I don't think it made me hate them any less, but it was just different.

I followed her, grabbed her. I tore off her clothes and found the black stains of Rasputin's hands on her pale body. He had fondled her breasts and stomach. The black tar was growing like ice along her body. I tried to stop it. I tried to keep her away from it. I tried.

Recruitment

I wandered the streets for hours and hours. I didn't want to stop walking. I walked and walked. As I walked down the street, I heard the words "prince," "Rasputin" and "assassinate" one million times. The streets and buildings seemed to whisper it as I passed.

Everyone looked at me as though I bore the mark of Cain. They couldn't have known I was involved. I couldn't even be sure they knew anything at all. Most people didn't know my face or my name. I can't be like Cain. I am purging evil, not causing it. I'm getting rid of the man who has his black-stained hand on the throat of the tsar. But what if that's what Cain thought?

I found a nice quiet place where I could be alone. I took my sack from my back and grabbed a palm full of sugar. I poured what was in my hand into a cup and covered it with my palm to keep the wind from carrying it away.

I walked into my tavern. I went up to the owner and placed the cup with the sugar in it on his table.

"What will this get me?" I asked. He stuck his finger in the cup and put it in his mouth.

"Sugar? A couple meals."

"A couple?" I said, hoping to sway him into giving me three.

"I'm sorry. There isn't enough here for an entire batch."

"A batch of what?"

"A batch of anything."

"Deal." We shook hands, and he poured the sugar into a jar. Then he brought me a meal. It was cold and slimy.

"There is some news floating around. The prince is going to kill the Rasputin man," he whispered.

"Who?"

"I have heard it from different people at different times of the day."

I passed by a school where the children were lining up outside of the small brick building. The schoolteacher was trying to organize them into two rows. They were singing a song about how the prince had killed Rasputin. It was a familiar tune, but I couldn't remember the name. At this point, I wouldn't be surprised if they printed a headline in the newspaper that Rasputin was dead.

I knocked at the silk bastard's home. The little servant answered.
"He's not in at the moment," he said. I grabbed the door.
"Where is he?" I asked.
"I'm afraid I can't tell you that," he said, tilting his head back.
"Maybe you just need a moment to think."

The cab stopped, and I paid him with the servant's money. I spotted the silk bastard's automobile on the corner down the block from the party. The house was like a flame in the middle of a lake. Laughter and music. I walked up to the silk bastard's driver.

He recognized me and invited me to sit with him. I closed the door and leaned up against the seat cushion. It was very nice to sit, like the nails were being removed from my skin. I gave him some bread. The wind shook me. The driver's portion of the car wasn't covered, so we were out in the cold. I melted into the frame of the door. My elbow served as my cushion.

The silk bastard walked to the automobile with a reckless stagger. His shirt and jacket were dirty with expensive wine and food. He knew that they would be cleaned tomorrow.

I opened the door for him. He stumbled into the backseat. I climbed in after him and shut the door. He didn't see me sitting opposite him inside until he lit his cigarette. He dropped the lighter in his lap, burning himself.

"Who the hell are you! Driver!"
"Be quiet," I said, picking up the lighter from the floor of the cab.
"Who in the hell are you?" he yelled.
"Please don't scream. You will let the demons know where we are," I said in a whisper.

"Who are you?" he asked in a drunken slur.

"I'm your best friend," I said with daggers.

"Oh really? How extravagant." He finally discovered it was me and relaxed into his seat.

"How could you be so careless?"

"How would you like me to have you shot?" he asked with a stammer.

I flicked the lighter on and held it so he could light his cigarette. Before I held it to him, I made sure the flame revealed the knife in my lap.

The lighter was gold with his initials and seal engraved into the side. I put it in my pocket next to the one I had stolen from the British man.

"You are putting all of us in danger. I'm giving you an opportunity to help the tsar and his people. Why are you telling everyone who is going to try and kill him, and where?" It was difficult to speak. I felt like I had rocks in my mouth, and my own words were putting me to sleep.

"He is a degenerate necromancer," the silk bastard said, gripping his cane as a scared boy would grab his mother's leg. "We could kill him in the square at midday, and no one would care. They might even cheer us on." He actually believed that. He believed everything he said and did had the support of the entire country just because he was born as the Grand Duke.

"I don't know what that means," I said.

"Do we have a plan?"

"Yes."

"Why don't you just do it?" he asked. "Everyone already thinks it will be the prince."

"No, you have to do it," I said. He didn't sense the urgency of the situation.

"What is your plan?"

"Invite Rasputin to a party. Tell him there will be women. He can't refuse an invitation of any woman, especially virtuous, pale noblewomen." Tar on her breasts. "When he arrives, you poison him. You can poison the wine; he has an obvious weakness for it. With the devil destroyed, you become the savior of the family and the hero of the people. Then you can fondle the tsar's daughter between her legs and cry like a real man."

I could see a vain smile open onto his face like wooden gears cranking.

"About this poison business. Isn't poison a rather cowardly way to dispatch an enemy?" he asked.

"Yes, it is. You could borrow my knife, if you prefer."

"Perhaps you're right. Poison is probably the most efficient way. Besides, I have already secured someone to supply the poison."

"Secured?" I asked.

"I have recruited another person to our crusade."

"How many people do you plan to involve in this?"

"As many as it takes."

"It only takes one to kill a man," I told him. "No more people."

"I won't need anymore," he said confidently.

"We all need to meet to go over our plan," I said as I opened the door and exited the cab.

"That may be difficult to arrange. Perhaps later next week."

"No!" I slammed my fist against the metal of the door. The cool metal flexed and reverberated. "Tomorrow. Arrange it."

I closed the door and knocked on the hood of the car, waving to the driver as I passed by.

I wandered the streets all night. If I kept walking, I wouldn't fall asleep. When I saw day begin again, I began to walk to the Duke. I arrived at the silk bastard's home the following night. The servant opened the door, keeping his weak hand behind it.

"He is on his way outside now. Please wait in the automobile."

I waited. I might have fallen asleep a couple times.

Finally, the silk bastard emerged and had the servant drape a dark cape over his back. He stumbled to the automobile, and the driver tucked him into the seat.

"Push on," the silk bastard called out to the driver. He held his head, hungover.

The silk bastard took a white cigarette from his gold case, then searched his pockets for his lighter. I leaned in and lit it for him. When he was done, I made sure to show him that I had taken his lighter.

"That is mine."

"I know. It even has your name and seal on it." I put it in my pocket and leaned back. He suddenly understood.

We drove and drove. The automobile was fast and loud, like a parade. I crouched down and covered my face.

Hot, dizzy and sick. The driver said something, and the automobile stopped. I lifted my head. We were at the main entrance of the prince's palace. There were ranks of servants in line to bow to the silk bastard as he entered.

It was larger than the tsar's Winter Palace. It overlooked the Moika River and was a pale yellow color. White columns held up the entrance, and metal gates blocked off the commoners.

I approached the guards and showed them my official papers from my right front jacket pocket. They looked them over and whispered to each other.

"Do you have any weapons?" the guard asked, handing me my papers.

I handed him my knife and my wooden leg.

"What is that?" the guard asked, pointing to the string that held my sack to my back. "Let's have a look."

They took the torn sack from me and unrolled it. The guards lowered themselves onto their knees and ran their hands all over my food. They laughed and showed my things to each other. They watched me and jeered as I gathered up all my cheap things into my sack.

I followed the silk bastard into the palace by trailing his perfume. Everything was blurry. These gilded mazes were becoming exhausting. I needed a jar to break.

The silk bastard entered a giant hall and was met with loud greetings and clapping. It was a marble cave with gold and silver dripping down the walls. The gold trim could have bought enough food to feed the world for a year. Proper food, not thinned-out soup and fried dough, but meat and sweet tea.

There was a large table at the center surrounded by standing attendants and servants. The prince and a bald man with glasses were enjoying a meal.

The silk bastard and the prince were shaking hands, hugging and kissing each other's cheeks. The prince wore a white military tunic with metals and buttons. Buttons, buttons. Oh, glorious buttons. Golden bullet holes all down his chest. He was so happy that he was clapping and smiling.

I was not introduced to anyone or offered a seat at the table, which could hold forty people on one side. They went on laughing and clapping with each other as though I wasn't in the room. I stood behind the silk bastard. He sat very close to the prince.

"You look a little rough today," the prince said to the silk bastard.

"I think I was too ambitious last night," the silk bastard said.

"You are too ambitious every night." They laughed together for a few minutes. Their laughs rolled together like young pups playing with each other.

"Shall we get to it?" the silk bastard asked.

"Very well, if we must. Let us discuss the business at hand," the prince agreed. He had a thin, confident voice that I instantly wanted to choke.

"Very well," the silk bastard repeated. They spent almost ten minutes saying "very well" to each other. "Are we all still in agreement on the date?"

"Yes, about that -- it might be more convenient to postpone it until after the New Year."

"I am still under the impression that sooner is better than later," the silk bastard said.

"I simply can't do it until after this month," the bald man said. He had a nasal, flat voice. The three men began mindlessly saying dates and talking about parties. It sounded like three calendar books being shuffled together.

"Can you men truly not spare one evening to do your duty?" I said. They had the attention and focus of dimwitted children.

"Who is this man who speaks without permission?" the prince asked. He actually didn't know I was in the room until I spoke.

"He is our consultant on this matter," the silk bastard said. He was almost whispering to the prince.

"Oh, very well. How do we begin?" he asked. He burned his mouth on his tea and spilled a little on his tunic. He rang his little bell and ordered his attendant to come in. "Go on," he said, waving his hand at me, giving me permission to continue.

"He is very clever, so --" I immediately stopped when the attendant entered with his napkins. The attendant fussed over the prince like a toddler's mother, doing his best to clean the area around him and fill his cup with tea. The prince stomped his feet while the attendant cleaned because he wanted more tea.

"Go on then," the prince said. I stood in silence looking down at my boots. "I said you could go on!" I was looking at this fool as hard as I could. "Oh, for heaven's sake, that will be all," he said, forcing his teacup onto the attendant. I looked at the prince until the door was completely shut.

"You must lure Rasputin," I told the prince.

"I beg your pardon?" the prince replied without looking at me, sipping his tea. "I am a prince -- I don't need to lure anyone. It is their honor to receive an audience at my pleasure."

"This man does have a point," the bald man said. "We must leave nothing to chance. Remember, he is not a normal man, but a degenerate and a bastard. He may not be as receptive to your grace's most honorable invitations." I looked down and saw the bald man's cigarette case. I tried to think of ways I could take it so that I would have items from everyone. It would have been so much better if it were a lighter. I guess nothing is perfect.

I shifted my weight and felt something warm and wet run down my leg from my hip. I wanted to take the pressure off my side, but I didn't want to sit with these bastards. The blood and pus was collecting in my boot.

"He is very clever and won't just jump into a carriage to see you. He is a leopard. He'll return to his den. Wine and women. Bait. We are hunting, and wine is our bait. Wine and women," I said. I couldn't start any of my thoughts, only finish them. "Send a letter to Rasputin saying your wife wishes to meet him."

"I am not offering my wife to anyone."

"No, you are not offering her to him," the silk bastard said, hoping to calm the prince down. "He is like a leopard. We must bait him."

"I'm a prince. I'm not just going to offer my wife to some peasant."

"It is like bait. He can't refuse an invitation of any woman, especially a woman as beautiful and noble as your wife. We can poison the wine -- he has a weakness for wine and other fine things. He will have a taste of the poison wine and expire. Simple and effective," the silk bastard said. It was a very familiar plan. Almost as if I had thought of it.

"Very well, as long as he doesn't see my wife."

"No, she doesn't even have to be in the palace."

"Very well, well said, sir. That is a terrific plan. It is almost poetic; he shall die by the agency of his own sins. Beautiful."

"I have procured cyanide," the bald man said. He produced a bottle from his coat pocket and put it on the table. It was a fist-sized dark brown bottle with no label.

"You just carrying that around with you?" I asked.

"Yes, what else would I do?"

"If you get a drop of that on your finger or thigh, you could kill yourself," I told him. His eyes opened wide, and his spectacles fell onto the table on top of the poison bottle. He reached to grab his spectacles but then realized that they had touched the cyanide bottle. He took out his handkerchief and frantically began to wipe them down. He returned his spectacles to his head and realized he was holding the handkerchief that could have poison on it. He threw it on the table and held his hands out, fingers spread apart, with a frightened look on his face.

"Very well. It is settled," said the silk bastard. "I can send him my automobile to collect him on the night. We shall perform the deed in December and reap the praise all before we celebrate Christmas."

"Very well. I shall offer an invitation to my palace at the hand of my wife."

"Very well," said the silk bastard.

"Very well," said the prince.

The porter stepped out of the building without his coat.

"He wants to see you."

"Did he say why?" I asked.

"No."

I was so tired of walking up and down those damned stairs. I lived a quarter of my life walking those stairs. Every flight took five months from my life.

When I got to the top, I rested for a moment. I knocked, and the door creaked open.

The entire floor was filled with papers and soiled bandages from his filthy chest wound. The odor made me ill. Rasputin sat by the fire, flipping through files and letters. Every so often, he came upon a piece of paper and tossed it into the fire. He used a bandage to sop up the slime leaking from his chest and tossed it into the fire. Tongues of flame lapped toward his hand. Once the paper hit the flame, it grew and licked the heat from the walls. It spit the letters out the chimney in black coughs. He was feeding the beast, giving it life with his words and pus.

I crept into the room, and he turned his head immediately. He could smell me thinking. The yellow fire made his eyes sink back in his head.

"I wanted you to know that I have accepted an invitation to the prince's palace on the 16th. Now you will know where I'll be, so you won't have to panic, searching the city for me." There was a sober seriousness to him that made him even more vulgar.

"Thank you," I said. I worried that he might think I was involved. "Aren't you worried about accepting this invitation? There are rumors that they're going to try and assassinate you."

"There are always rumors about my assassination. If I took them all seriously, then I would have to remain inside forever."

"These are serious rumors."

"It would be very improper for me to refuse an invitation by the prince. Our fates are in God's hands. Besides, I know these men. They don't have the will to kill me. The prince even tried to seduce me, the bastard."

I didn't know if he was telling the truth or bragging.

"It's cold," he said as he handed me an envelope. "That is for you." I looked into the envelope and saw money. "You can tell a horse's health by its teeth." He tossed another piece of paper into the fire. "I want you to mail that letter as soon as possible. The money is for you, for running the errand."

I looked at the letter and saw that it was addressed to the tsar.

"This isn't necessary," I said, trying to hand the money back to him.

"It is, though," he replied. He did not take the envelope back but continued to look through the papers on the floor. "And here -- I think this belongs to you."

He handed me the watch that I had left in his apartment. I tried to keep from shaking as I took it. The fire was trying to bite me. I could hear the flies gathering. I backed out of the room and closed the door as he tossed another crimped page into the red fire.

I took the letter down to the post station and entered the telegram office. I approached the clerk and asked, "Has he received or sent any telegrams?"

"Just this," he said, handing me a telegram from the special file.

I have given the Church Father the balance of all of my accounts. Contact him in a month's time. He is to use 2000 rubles to pay for repairs in the church, and the other is to go to my wife and children. When the repairs are complete, will you give my family the balance and then settle up with the Church Father the next time you see him?

You may have 100 rubles for your trouble. My thanks to you, and may God bless you a thousand times.
    -Rasputin

    He appears to be making his arrangements, getting affairs in order. Does he know? I handed the telegram back to the clerk and left. The telegram weighed on me as much as a boulder would. Can he see?

    I could still smell his foul odor. I covered my nose, but it was coming from me. I took off my coat and my bandage. My wound was black and red and purple. It was moist and smelled like death. With my black soot-stained hand, I immediately tossed the bandage to the street and hurried away from it.

    Black hands and rotting from the inside out. He had infected me. He touched me, and I watched him, and now I have the black hands and the putrid sores. Rasputin must die soon before there is nothing left of me.

Night of the Murder

Around midday, I was relieved by one of my men. I entered the tavern and stomped my feet. No darting eyes. I pulled the owner to a private corner.

"I need a favor."

"What?"

"Tell people I was here all night."

"Who would ask?"

"Anyone." I handed him my sack. He unrolled it, and his eyes lit up at the sight of the sugar, salt and what was left of the flour.

"All of this for telling people you were here all night?" he asked.

"And this." I punched him in the face with my bare fist. He fell back and grabbed his nose. He was bleeding and swearing. Everyone in the tavern turned to look at us. He collected himself and punched me back in the eye.

"What the hell was that for?" he asked as he picked me up by the throat.

"I need more evidence that I was here. More than just your word." He threw me down and put his sleeve to his nose to stop the bleeding.

"You could have warned me."

"I don't think you would've let me do it."

"Probably not." He rolled up the food and walked back toward the kitchen. I waited. Once people settled down and stopped looking over at me, I quietly slipped out the back door.

The cold air. My bruised eye. My infected knife wound. I hobbled to the prince's home. No carriage, no witness. No ride in an automobile. No chances. I staggered and stumbled. The pain. The fatigue. The pain.

The terrible smell. The hunger. The ivy. The black hands. The firing squad. The priest and his dirty beard.

    The prince's palace looked like it was dissolving into fog. I could feel the hole in my side, and my feet burned. A breeze from the river flew up and slapped me in the face. The attendants pointed to places I couldn't see. I must be nobler.

    I walked to the side entrance. My bruised feet crumbled away like rough bread. I almost had to break a thin attendant's finger to keep his hand off my coat. The halls were golden, wide and hot.

    "Please follow me," I think he said. I grabbed his coattail so I didn't have to keep my eyes open. I followed him around the winding corridors and stairs.

    I was led into a glowing sitting room. The ceiling vaulted to the purple sky. There were two large windows that blinked into the courtyard. The candles on the wall wept creamy wax. There were tables, liquor bottles and ashtrays. Golden mountain ranges.

    Three men huddled around the large fire. The walls melted in books and portraits.

    As the door closed, my three confederates turned. It was beneath them to offer hospitality. The angels and I tightened our armor.

    The bald man and the silk bastard sat at the table, sucking air nervously though their pale cigarettes. The prince paced about the room clumsily, drinking in small careful sips. All the practiced confidence had eaten through them like salt. Now they just sniffed at me with condescending fright.

    "He wouldn't give his name, sir," the servant complained.

    "That is quite fine. Please inform me when our guest arrives."

    "Yes, sir," the servant said, bowing before he left.

    "Is everything set?" I asked. My gravelly voice cut the air like a horn.

    "It's all ready," the silk bastard said. "My automobile just left to pick him up."

    "In this room, here?" I asked.

    "No, I have prepared a special room for him."

    "Show me."

I tumbled slowly down the stairs to see the cellar where the prince planned to serve Rasputin. More stairs. Everything that hurts and everything I hate is at the end of stairs. I couldn't lift my leg. We descended sideways and upside down.

The room was small, with an arched ceiling and curved walls. A table was set in the middle of the room for three. The table sprouted sweet cakes and wine. It reminded me of a prostitute's dress.

"Each cake has enough cyanide baked into it to kill a man. The wine is also mixed with poison," the prince said. He leaned toward the silk bastard and whispered something. The silk bastard shook his head, and the prince leaned forward again.

"Who baked these? Did you?" I asked.

"Of course not," he snorted and laughed.

"Who baked the cakes?"

"My kitchen staff, of course."

"You had your cook bake murder cakes?"

I looked at the table and saw that it was only set for three. "Do you entertain down here frequently?" I asked. Something seemed very peculiar about the room.

"No, I had this room prepared especially for tonight."

"Then your entire house knows you're killing someone tonight."

"I don't like your tone, peasant," the prince said. I was going to send my pipe across his arm, but I couldn't find it. The silk bastard leaned close to me and whispered.

"Don't say 'kill' -- it makes him nervous."

The sitting room. I found glass eyes on the wall. The cool air burrowed its way through the panes. "How long?" I asked.

"I would say half an hour," the silk bastard said.

"You must hide behind the curtain," the prince instructed. I could barely hear him.

"We will just wait." The palace heat worked its way through the cold I brought from the street. It was beginning to make me sweat. The heat was a wagon on my chest. I won't hide behind a curtain, and I won't remove my coat. That's how the devil infects you. He uses the black hands to remove discomfort. He's not getting my goddamn coat. My side was throbbing with pain. Can the devil enter through my hip wound? I stuck my finger in my hip to keep the spirits out. I hurt so bad that I almost vomited.

"Your guest is here," the servant announced.

The prince set his glass down and fixed his coat and shirt. The men all shook hands and kissed cheeks and cleared throats. I could feel him turn toward me. I turned into a shadow on a lake. They could see me, but they had no idea who I was. The prince slumped out of the room like a boy summoned by his angry mother.

So many books in this room. How do you read inside out? The chill from the glass released something inside me. I could feel the archangels. Their hands caressed my face, giving me strength in this den of dragons, demons and liars. For the first time in 145 years, I closed my eyes and felt.

I awoke flexing every muscle in my body. The prince burst into the room, yelping like a little dog. "Something's wrong!"

"What?" I asked.

"He's eating the cakes and wine with the poison, but nothing's happing. He's been down there eating them for an hour."

"Are you certain the poison is lethal, or in a lethal dose?" the silk bastard asked.

"Yes, I consulted a doctor earlier."

"You consulted a doctor?" I couldn't believe it. "Perhaps the rumors you spread will kill him."

"Stop saying 'kill'!" the prince yelled.

"What do we do?" screamed the silk bastard.

"Do you have a pistol?" I asked.

"Yes," said the prince frantically.

"Get it," the silk bastard said.

"Good idea," the prince said. He rang a bell, and a servant promptly appeared. "Fetch my pistol." The servant scampered off. I was surprised he hadn't ordered his servant to kill Rasputin. The prince ran his hands through his sweating hair. His fingers were dissolving.

The servant brought the pistol, and the prince loaded it. He grabbed the pistol with his thumb and finger. He presented it to me.

"You," I told him.

"What?" His eyes bulged like a dead horse's. I grabbed him by the arm and pulled him toward me. He had a thin, rail-like body. I felt my hand sizzle as I squeezed him.

"Find your courage, boy," I told him. "Do your duty. Do it easier. Do it quick. I have no more pockets."

He was surprised how heavy the pistol was. He held it like it was a cobra that coiled around his hand. The snake seemed to squeeze it so hard that it made his entire arm shake. Squeezed and squeezed. I took my hand back, and he had one last drink before he marched away.

I opened the eyes and felt the iced air freeze and harden my coat and body. I knew that after the prince had taken the snake out of his pocket, I would be forced to descend into the cellar and see what devils drink to. The wind from outside was punching out the fire and slapping my head.

"Close the window," the silk bastard ordered. I used my hand and pushed it completely open, sliding the curtain back. The wind hit the curtain like a sail, and the room began to turn. The book pages flapped from the wind and turned to ice, and all the knowledge was now like glass.

"Peasant," the silk bastard murmured to himself.

The bald man charged me. "Did you not hear the Grand Duke?" he asked. I hit him on the side of the face with my elbow.

"You bastard! I will have you executed!" the silk bastard said.

I tossed my knife across the room onto the table next to the silk bastard. The hard metal shattered the glasses and chipped the wooden top. The men looked at the knife. It dissolved into sand and was falling through the cracks in the floor. Everything was blurry, but I looked straight into the silk bastard's eyes.

I walked closer, and they stepped backward into the hard wall. I began to slap and punch. "You can't do a damned thing," I told him. Joyous. I punched and choked. I felt my pants become wet from the blood of my hip wound. The book pages flapped again.

The prince slammed into the room. "I did it! I did it!" The pistol was smoking, and his hands were shaking. He leaned against a chair to catch his breath.

"Tell me exactly what happened."

"When I approached the bottom of the stairs, I saw him. He was standing, facing a crucifix on the opposite wall. I told him to pray, and then I shot him. The whole business was quite thrilling." He gently placed the pistol on the chair and rubbed his hands, sore from the gun recoil.

"Good work, my man. The deed is done," the silk bastard said. The excitement made him peel away from the wall and into the prince's arms.

"It was so pure. Can we get someone to close that window?" the prince asked.

I closed the window. Silence. The devil might be looking for a new body to take. In my mind, I saw paper fingers over a fire. I could hear the prince and the silk bastard whispering.

"Take me to him," I demanded as I walked toward the chair and grabbed the pistol.

"Where?" the prince asked.

"To see him."

"Why?"

"To make sure he's dead," I answered. I took a handful of ammunition from a small metal tin that the servant had brought.

We entered the black cellar. There was an annoying song skipping on the gramophone. The prince pointed at Rasputin's body like a bird dog.

"Vanquished," he chirped. "I even did it while he was looking at the crucifix on the mantel."

"Good thinking," I said reluctantly. "Are you sure he's dead?"

"Of course he's dead; I shot him three times," he said. He tried to roll him over onto his back. Rasputin had rooted his dead body into the stone floor. While the prince struggled, I looked at the table that had been set for him. Many of the poisoned cakes had been eaten, and the poison-laced wine was gone. With all the poison he consumed, even if the prince hadn't shot him, he would have been dead soon anyway.

The prince turned the dead Rasputin onto his back. I looked at the still body and laughed. Spiders were already spinning webs in his beard. I leaned over the shoulder of the prince to look at the closed eyes. Just then, Rasputin's eyes burst open, and he grabbed the throat of the prince.

"You bad boy," he said as he began to strangle the prince. His eyes were red and bulging as they tried to escape from his head. The prince jumped back and pushed me against the wall. My head hit the mantel, and I fell. Everything went black. I heard the prince yelling, "He's still alive! He's still alive! I shot him three times, and he's still alive. He tried to choke me." The prince ran up the stairs.

I closed my eyes and couldn't hear anything.

I awoke flexing every muscle in my body. I heard a thundering sound and popped the stitches in my eyes. There was that odd and annoying song still playing on the gramophone. I could smell the cakes, pus and candle wax.

Rasputin was gone. I opened the pistol. It had three shots left. The prince had actually shot him three times. After my eyes adjusted to the darkness of the room, I could see the trail of blood. Rasputin had used that red current to escape from the cellar.

The prince and the silk bastard entered the room and gasped. They looked around frantically.

"What do we do?" the prince cried.

"I thought you shot him," the silk bastard said.

I followed the blood trail out the door and into the courtyard outside. The sky held a fog above the city. There were lights from the street lamps below and stars and the moon from above. Everything glowed like a church window. The saints and angels must have pulled the screen to save God from the sight of it all. I could see him all the way across the courtyard.

Rasputin was dragging himself, slithering along the wet, cold ground. The heat from his body turned to black steam in the cold air. I lifted my pistol and fired. The devil dropped after the third shot. Empty black smoke was still rising from his body, like evil souls evaporating into the night. Noxious vapor choked the sky.

I sprinted and found him rolling in pain and confusion. I waited for him to die, but he only become stronger. He threw himself around, then began to crawl after me. I slowly backed up. He kept crawling.

I collected some bullets from my pocket, cracked open the cobra and began to feed it. I backed up while the cobra kept spitting out my bullets onto the ground. He kept crawling. He grabbed my foot, and I fell onto the ground. He used my body to pull himself up like a cat until his face was up against mine. Blood and black pus dripped onto me. His body was warm, and his breath had the smell of rotting garbage. His eyes were open so wide that I could see the empty space between his eyes.

He grabbed my head and pulled me even closer to him. "You naughty boy." He put his hands on my neck and tried to choke me. He was trying to eat me with his eyes. I grabbed the side of his body and squeezed as hard as I could. Slimy, hot liquid flowed onto my hand. I could feel his stomach seize as he screamed in pain from his wounds.

I got my knee under him and rolled his body off mine. I stood, pulled on the snake and watched. Then I shot him in the head. Blood flowed into his eyes and hair. The prince and the Grand Duke had made their way toward me. I wrapped the body in my coat and told them to pick up his feet.

"I'll call for a driver."

"No, we can't dispose of a body in your coach. No witnesses. We'll dump him in the river." After wondering if they should keep their gloves on or off, they reluctantly bent down and helped me heave the body.

We marched through the side street. The ground bowed beneath our steps. Then the body let out a moan, and my two helpers let go of his legs. The full weight of the body fell onto me. The coat tore on my side, and I grunted. There was now heat running down my leg. The body was still warm, and I could hear the devil gasping quietly. He was still alive. I dropped him out of shock and stumbled to the ground.

"We must hurry," I said.

We reached the edge of the water. I grabbed Rasputin's belt and used it to tie a rock to his legs. The river had collected ice under the bridge. I grabbed a rock and flung it over to break the ice. I lifted the body to toss it over the side. I swung the limbs over the ledge one after the other. He seemed to have seven arms and seven legs. The body was hot but lifeless, and it smelled of burning manure. The devil was still shoveling coal in Rasputin's black furnace.

I rolled him into the water, and he began to sink.

His body floated to the surface. He was moving. His head was bobbing in and out of the water. I couldn't understand him, but it sounded as if he was reciting a prayer and blessing us with his hand. He sunk down under the water like an old potato in soup.

Silence.

A chunk of ice began to shift up and down. He was melting the ice.

I grabbed the lantern that the silk bastard was using and tossed it down onto the thin sheet of ice. Rasputin was digging and clawing to escape through the frozen water. His eyes were red from the blood and the cold water, and he looked straight into me. I knew that once some fool has put me out of my misery, I will be forced to meet him again. He disappeared down into the dark, cold water. The fire from the lantern was consumed by the cold ice. I listened to the black flowing water in the dark.

A Broken Accord

I awoke flexing every muscle in my body. I shut the window. My entire body was in pain. I had terrible dreams and wonderful visions. I fell asleep in my dream and had to wake up twice. All I could see in my mind were the bloody bulging eyes of Rasputin.

I was in my own apartment. I didn't remember walking here last night. The room had become smaller. It was empty and cold. I put my coat over my head and tried to gather the energy to change my bandage.

Even though I was exhausted, I felt as though I were awake. I could suddenly start paying attention.

I hobbled to Rasputin's apartment.

"Report."

"He left around eight at night and hasn't returned."

"Did you follow him?"

"Yes. I followed him to the prince's palace. The Grand Duke's automobile picked him up. I didn't stay outside the palace grounds and returned to wait for him here."

"Good. You are relieved." He left, and I stood watching a room that will never be filled. It was waiting for someone who will never return. The building seemed lighter and brighter with the haze of Rasputin evaporated. Yet in the distance, there was still a dark and fierce cloud. It was on its way toward us, and no one could stop it. I leaned my head against the building, shifted my weight to my good side and went back to sleep.

Rasputin's body was fished out of the river three days later. I was asked to go to the hospital to observe the body for the final pages of my report. His body was frozen and contorted. His arms were extended from his frame, frozen in place. He had tried to climb out of the icy water. The grease from his hair mixed with the water to form a black sludge that dripped down the wooden stretcher. The knife wound on his chest was still discharging black pus, and he smelled horrible. Although it was unmistakably him, it didn't look like him. With his eyes closed, he looked like a water-damaged portrait. Without those eyes, he would have no power or allure.

I put my hand into my pocket and found a letter. It was the sealed letter to the tsar. Rasputin had given it to me, and I hadn't mailed it. The envelope was still greasy from his fingers.

I pulled out my leather pouch from my jacket's right inner pocket and took out my tool. I squeezed the edges with my fingers, inserted the long metal rod and pulled out the letter. I felt as though he was there listening to me. I put the letter close to my face and read.

I write and leave behind me this letter at St. Petersburg. I feel that I shall leave life before January 1st.

I wish to make known to the Russian people, to Papa, to the Russian Mother and to the children, to the land of Russia, what they must understand. If I am killed by common assassins, and especially by my brothers the Russian peasants, you, Tsar of Russia, have nothing to fear, remain on your throne and govern, and you, Russian Tsar, will have nothing to fear for your children; they will reign for hundreds of years in Russia. But if I am murdered by boyars, nobles, and if they shed my blood, their hands will remain soiled with my blood... for twenty-five years, they will not wash their hands of my blood. They will leave Russia.

Brothers will kill brothers, and they will kill each other and hate each other, and for twenty-five years, there will be no nobles in the country. Tsar of the land of Russia, if you hear the sound of the bell that will tell you that Rasputin has been killed, you must know this: If it was your relations who have wrought my death, then no one of your family, that is to say, none of your children or relations, will remain alive for more than two years. They will be killed by the Russian people...I shall be killed. I am no longer among the living.

Pray, pray, be strong, think of your blessed family.
-Rasputin

He knew his death was coming. He prepared for it. He left a trap for the future. A trap that history will eventually stumble into. I rolled the letter around the tool and returned it to its sealed envelope.

I gave the letter to the post office worker and bribed him to backdate it a few days before the night he died. The letter left a cold chill down my side. It felt dirty and dreadful. It was like realizing someone had been watching you outside your window.

I returned to headquarters. I didn't bother to hide my limp. Everyone was too busy to notice. We no longer focused on union or labor organizers, but revolutionaries.

Everything was all wrong. I no longer belonged or the lights were different. I expected a feeling, a great consuming sense of accomplishment and fulfillment. But I felt nothing.

I didn't feel anything. I didn't feel happiness, relief, understanding, completion, satisfaction, pride or… I couldn't even think of the word that was the opposite of loneliness. It should have the word "happy" in it, but I can't think of the word. Maybe I'll remember it when I feel it.

I walked into the clerk's office to collect my new orders. He looked over his papers at me and lifted his mouth. I never forgot how much I hated him. I remember always wanting to hurt him, but right now, I felt numb.

"What do you want?" he asked sharply.

"To collect my orders."

"Your orders? Your orders? You know, we are supposed to put together a list of the best men whom we feel should be reassigned to the front. Would you like those orders? Would you like to be assigned to the front?"

"Have I been assigned to the front?"

"You didn't answer my question," he said. I knew that the rent he would want would be very expensive. He would just keep taking and keep taking. Then when I had nothing, he would put me on a list and send me to the front. He would just take it all and send me to the front.

"You didn't answer my question," I told him. He was stunned, and his mouth curved.

"I beg your pardon? Who do you think you're talking to, you dirty beggar?" I turned my back on him and walked to the door. "I will have you against a wall for this. Who do you think you are talking to?" He began to twitch and fidget. His eyes darted back and forth, and I could smell his sweat, like sugar.

I had lived my life up until that point like a stowaway on a ship. I knew I needed to get off the ship

It didn't matter anymore. I didn't care if I was sent to the front. At least then I knew that I would die soon, and the empty pain would be over.

"Where do you think you are going?"

"I don't know." I turned and left.

He leaned back in his chair. I could hear the chair squeak so hard that I thought it would break.

"How dare you!" he screamed. "You have been assigned to the front! Signed the papers myself. You vermin!"

He was going to make me pay to stay off this list when I was already on it. I didn't care anymore. At least at the front, it will be quick and easy. I thought the afternoon would be perfect; perhaps I could even get some sleep.

As I sat on my floor, going through my post, I wondered what it would be like at the front. I had heard terrible stories about fighting in the snow with no ammo, no guns and no shoes. Nobles couldn't dress themselves without their servants, let alone manage the army. Fighting for them is like standing in front of firing squad, except it's colder and takes longer. I would have to be sure to die as quickly as possible.

I don't know what I thought before Rasputin. I didn't think, I suppose. I was too snow-blind by the garbage around me to notice how rotten everything was. I'm tired of living in their garbage and being forced to tell them how great it smells. Tired of having people spit in my face.

When I returned the following day, the office was in a panic.

"I have something for you," called a voice from behind me. I turned around and saw another bureaucrat. He handed me an envelope with his little hand. "New orders."

I opened the envelope. I had been reassigned from the front to assignments here in the city.

I was assigned to locate and arrest the leaders of one of the many protests, strikes and demonstrations. It wouldn't be too difficult; the protestors were still not very organized. They were, however, very fierce. They had gone from union organizers to revolutionaries. They had gone from asking for concessions to demanding them.

My orders were to find the leaders and kill them and their families.

I watched a protest from some distance for a couple of days. My hip had almost healed. I still walked with a limp, but the smell was going away. My hands were still black.

They were marching back and forth, up and down the square. They waved torn banners and yelled. Even though they were all chanting the same slogans, they were not shouting as one. There were just so many of them. They were women, children, old men, young men, even the dogs barked in protest. We could no more stop this demonstration than chase a storm away. We could only take cover and try to wait it out.

I watched the outside of the crowd and looked for runners. In large crowds, there is only one way to spread information: through people. These people run up and down, delivering messages and orders. Once I could identify two or three of these runners, I followed them. They would lead me to one runner, then to another and then another. It was like following links in a chain.

I followed them back and back and back.

Finally I spotted him. I saw the runner who came from outside the crowd.

I tracked the runner by waiting for him at the edge of his route. Each time he would deliver a message, I would see the next section of the track he took. It only took a couple days of messages to find the building he was starting from. It was a few blocks from the crowds of people. The screams and chants could be faintly heard bouncing off the walls.

The building was four stories tall. It was old and pale. The walls were falling in on themselves, and all the wood had been stripped off for fuel. I didn't want to enter the building until dark.

I quietly entered. It was colder inside than outside, and it was deserted. There was a dripping sound.

I walked on the worn part of my soles to avoid any sound. I looked around the stairs and noticed the shadows of a dim lantern. There were five men collected around a small lantern. They had hung a blanket in the window to avoid giving away their position. The cigarette smoke and lantern exhaust filled the room with a haze. I took out my knife and wooden leg, and entered the room. They instantly froze. The larger one pulled out a knife.

"That won't be necessary," I said. "I'm not going to do anything to you." I put my knife and wooden leg on the ground. "When you have your runner go back and forth, have him take different routes. That will make it more difficult to find you. If you can, try and move around to different buildings."

"You're part of the special police," the tall one said.

"And one of you should stand guard. You can take turns."

"Do you want a cigarette?" he asked.

"Yes." He handed me a cigarette. I used the British man's gold lighter. We looked at each other for a long time. We smoked and coughed. They swayed back and forth, like trees hoping to fight off the cold.

"Why are you helping us, Special Police Okhrana Man?" he asked. I thought for a long time. I couldn't think of why I was helping them. I looked down and realized that I had begun to sway. "Would you be willing to help us some more?" he asked.

"Maybe."

"Are you crazy?" another man asked. "He's just trying to gain our confidence. We should kill him."

I put my hands in my pockets and waited for them to kill me and end the pain.

"Are you sent here to spy, Okhrana Man?" the tall one asked.

"Would you believe anything I say?" I asked.

"What can you do for us that would make us trust you?" he asked me.

"You want me to earn the favor of helping you?" I asked, laughing. "Thanks for the cigarette," I said as I turned to leave.

"Wait," he said. I turned around. "I don't think I can believe you," the tall one said. "But I think, in this case, the opportunity is worth the risk. What do you want?"

"I don't know." I said. I had no idea what I wanted or needed. I was just tired. I wanted it to be over.

"We are getting some resistance."

"I can imagine," I said.

"No, it isn't from the government or the police. It's something else. There is someone out there killing all of the leaders. Is that you?"

"No. We are supposed to bring you in for questioning before we kill you." They shuddered at the methodology. "Then we are supposed to kill your families."

I was questioned once.

"They don't arrest them -- they just seem to know what we are going to do next, and then they strike and set us back weeks."

"Almost like they know everything?" I asked.

"Exactly."

"Is there a woman who interacts with you or people around you? She is very confident and has a scar on this cheek."

"How do you know about her? She is one of the prostitutes who works in our tavern. What does she have to do with anything?"

"She is the reason your enemies know everything."

"She's just a woman!" the tall man said.

"Apparently she's much smarter than you," I said.

"She's dead," he said, spitting on the ground.

"Be careful -- she will have men protecting her."

"What do they look like?"

"I don't know. I killed the last two, so she probably has new ones." They smiled and laughed nervously.

"We do want your help."

"What do you want me to do exactly?" I asked.

"We would like you to take care of these people for us."

"Take care of them," I said. The very thought made me exhausted.

"We can pay you," the tall man said. He gave me a handful of half-smoked cigarettes.

"And now you have nothing," I said. I gave them back their cigarettes. "I want you and another man to meet me tomorrow. Bring a weapon."

"Where are we meeting you?" he asked with a quiver in his voice. I told him the address two or three times so that he would remember it. It was a crowded area a block from their tavern.

As I picked up my knife and wooden leg, I ran into the runner who skidded over himself and slammed into the doorframe. He looked at the others and wondered if I was going to arrest him. I helped him up and patted him on the back.

I arrived at the meeting place almost an hour early. I spotted the two men instantly. It was the tall man from yesterday and another lumbering fool.

"Where the hell have you been?" the other man asked.

"Did you bring weapons?" I asked the tall man, ignoring the other one.

"Yes." They each opened their coats and pulled out a section of a broom handle. I couldn't help but giggle.

"Alright, follow me -- and don't say a word." I led them to a spot across the street from the tavern.

"Why are we here so early? She doesn't arrive here until later in the evening," the other man said.

"So we aren't surprised by anything," I replied.

"What could possibly surprise us?" he asked. He was a thick man with a broad nose, dim eyes and terrible breath.

"What is your profession?" I asked.

"I'm a member of the people's party," he said.

"And before that?" I asked. He snarled at me.

"He used to make shoes," the tall man told me. I suddenly realized I was helping people who were no better than children. I turned back to the former shoemaker.

"I don't know what would surprise us. That's why it would be surprising," I told him. I don't think he understood.

We watched the tavern for hours. They had no patience.

I watched as broken people entered and left the tavern. I watched the sun go down. I watched the street fill and clear. I was tired of watching. Exhausted. Exhausted of standing outside. Exhausted of the city. Exhausted of the entire fucking life. I killed the devil, and now I want my peace.

The confident lady entered the tavern and stayed for hours. She was gathering information and making contacts. Even with that terrible scar down her cheek, she was extremely assured. I hated her for that. She had a ruined face, and she was still the most amazing person I ever saw. I destroyed Rasputin, and I barely had the will to walk here.

I grabbed the tall man and handed him my knife.

"I thought you were going to do it," he said.

"No," I said.

"Worried you will be in trouble with your people?" the former shoemaker asked hatefully. He was very unreasonable for someone who was receiving valuable help.

"No, he's right," the tall man said. "We have to do this ourselves. Besides, it will be more meaningful for the revolution."

"What if she has people to protect her?" the former shoemaker asked.

"She will," I told them. He took the knife. "You stay on this side of the tavern door, and you stay on the other." I took out one of my maps and flicked on the British man's lighter to see. I pointed. "We want to herd her down this street and into this alley. It is a dead end and quiet." I rolled up the map and put it back in my jacket. "When she comes out, you two make sure she walks east toward the river. When she gets to the alley, I'll be waiting for her, and then you take care of the other men. Everyone clear?" I asked. They nodded their heads while panting very hard.

The confident lady came out. She put her wrap over her head and started down the street. The tall man and the former shoemaker herded her and led her down the street. I was able to corral her in an alley.

When she saw me, her eyes opened wide. She hated me as much as I did. She pulled out a knife. I dropped my wooden leg on the ground and took off my coat. I raised my hands and closed my eyes, waiting for her to do her job. Nothing.

I opened my eyes. She was just looking at me.

"Go on," I said.

We heard the struggle of her men and my revolutionaries. She became startled and escaped by squeezing her small body through a missing plank in the wooden fence. She vanished into the darkness.

I heard the sound of footsteps running toward me. My revolutionaries came up to me shaking and blinking.

"What happened?"

"She got away," I said. I picked up my wooden leg and coat.

"Got away?" the former shoemaker screamed. He came at me with my knife.

"It's fine," the tall man said. "She isn't important."

The tall man kept the knife.

Over the next few weeks, I showed them how to avoid leaking sensitive information. I taught them how to send messages without being caught. They were fast learners and had many questions. Money was useless, except to burn for fuel. They also made sure to keep me in their circle. If they succeeded, they would have more questions for me. And when they need the people to go back to work, they will call on me.

I told them it would be fine. I was happy to tell anyone this information. I didn't want it. It was almost a relief to not have it anymore.

I gave them the name of my tavern, so they knew where they could find me if they ever needed anything. After I handed them the map, they all gave me their entire supply of cigarettes and each took turns smiling and bowing at me. They wanted to grab my arm or hug me, but in our new workers' state, no one is supposed to shake hands. I was never a gentleman, so I didn't have to worry about breaking that habit.

Bread Riots

Even though Rasputin was gone, the country was still very ill. It was as if he had been a gangrenous leg that we had amputated, but the country was still dying. I was called back to headquarters. My superior stood on the stairs like a politician, speaking to all the agents. This was only one of a few times I had ever seen him. I didn't remember what he looked like.

"There is to be rioting in the streets, you see. The guards and the Cossacks are being called in, and we are to be giving them support. The guard has given us firearms to be handed out. We are to report on the east side of the bridge and will be given more orders there, you see. Now I want you all to line up and sign for your pistol."

We lined up and inched slowly toward the superior who was handing out pistols. We were each given an old rusty firearm, a handful of ammunition and a pen to sign the register with.

As we approached the bridge, I saw the Cossack commander mounted on his large horse with his tall hat. He was yelling something to us, but I couldn't hear him, and I didn't have any motivation to obey him. I followed the man in front of me to the square.

"Line up and get ready, men," the Cossack commander said. He was riding his horse up and down the line, trying to rally those of us who were underfed and tired of all this. A mob of people began to inch close to us. Once the crowd approached, the commander couldn't be found. I couldn't even hear the loud footsteps of his horse. Even though they were coming toward us, I wasn't scared. I don't think any of us were scared. Dying here would be much easier than dying in the front, or being taken for questioning.

I saw the people in the mob and felt tired, hungry and sore. I dropped my gun and let the protesters pass me one at a time. When I looked around, I was astonished to see that the soldiers and militia had done the same. The protesters passed us, cheering and slapping our backs. One of them grabbed me and kissed my cheek.

They were so happy and angry and full of violent passion that it was like fuel being poured into a rusty motor.

They passed us and entered the building. The sounds of windows breaking, furniture smashing and people screaming were carried back to us by the wind. Even though Rasputin didn't create the poison between the common people and the nobles, he was the screw that opened the seal, spilling the venom of the people onto the ruling class.

I saw the protesters exit the building. They had crosses and icons in their hands. They threw them violently on the ground and began to set them on fire. The gold and silver were taken away by whoever could carry them. A priest, a noble and his wife were dragged out from the building. They were placed in front of the burning icons and beaten.

I sat down, hoping the mob would take me and end it. It would be welcomed, or at least, I wouldn't put up a fight. I'm so tired of the pain and loneliness. I just need it to end.

By the time the Cossacks commander rode back toward us, the people of quality were already dead. The fire in the street had died out, and the crowd had made off with most of the valuables. The building was like a dead cow, picked to the bone.

The leader of the Cossacks came toward me on his horse.

"What happened here?"

"Just what it looks like," I said. He took his sword and raked me over the head with it. I fell to the ground instantly and felt a warmness run down my scalp.

"You need to learn your place, you bastard," he said proudly. He didn't smell the fire or see the dead nobles in the street. He didn't understand that places were changing. I looked up at him as clearly as I could. My eyes began to water and went cross.

I awoke flexing every muscle in my body. That bastard didn't fucking kill me. I looked around and noticed that rioters surrounded me. They had taken me out of the street after they witnessed my beating. They had put a bandage on my head and were cheering me.

The revolutionaries took the pistols. They were old pistols, and the ammo was unreliable at best. Workers in the factories tampered with most ammunition. They had hoped it would stop the war or bring down the government. All it really did was cost some poor fool of a soldier his life in a trench. If the ammo hadn't been tampered with or was lucky enough not to misfire, it wouldn't travel straight to the target. The revolutionaries were happy to have them. I don't think they really knew how to use them effectively and would probably shoot off their own noses.

I sat in my tavern. They had no food or drink to buy, and the fire was only fueled by old protest pamphlets. All I could do was sit and wait. I had no idea what was going to happen; I just knew that something was going to happen.

I saw the British man enter the tavern. He sat down and threw his gloves on the table.

"Sometimes I just don't know what to make of you, old boy."

"Go away," I told him.

"I've seen it before, you know. Losing 'the will' and so forth."

"I never had 'the will'."

"Nonsense. You swiped her face with your knife. That was most willful. But then, this strange business in the alley. And aiding the revolutionaries. It doesn't all fit."

"I just gave people a little information."

"I've seen the kind of information you've given them," he said with a laugh.

"You got what you wanted. Why are you here?"

"Even if these people succeed, the tsar still has men, armies, who are loyal to the death. It will be civil war. Thousands more will die. Is that what you want? Do you have any idea what you've done? You have committed treason. That is punished by a firing squad."

"So is spying," I told him. He leaned back and calmed down a little.

"I'm not a spy."

"And I'm not a traitor."

"I see you're still keeping your journal. Is that the same one you kept while you guarded Rasputin? Why do you still have that?"

I didn't answer.

He continued, "Don't let your new friends read that. Who knows what they'll do to you." I put my journal in my pocket. "And if the tsar finds out what you did --"

"Have you been out in the streets lately?" I interrupted. "It isn't me who is in trouble. If anyone is in trouble, it's you. This is not your country.

You're a foreigner and the guest of the tsar. And you have overstayed your welcome."

"I just don't know what to make of you," he said, laughing again.

"I suppose you won't finish it for me."

"Afraid not, old boy. Not in my expertise. Besides, from what's coming, I think a better punishment for you is to live through every minute of it."

I tossed him his lighter.

He took it and tried to turn it on. It was out of fuel, and the flint was sticking. He shook it next to his ear and put it in his pocket. He stood and left.

Once things got worse, my new friends had even more questions. They wanted to know where things were. Before they destroyed my former headquarters, they moved all the files to a new building. They called this new building the headquarters.

They made a grand display of burning all the secret police files. When the cheers stopped, they had me help them set up the catalogue of all the copies of the burnt files in the new headquarters. Once they had a system up and running, I was approached by the tall man. He explained that they had appointed the former shoemaker to be the head of the new secret police. They wanted me to answer his questions and be his right-hand man. They wanted my journal. I ran fast as I could. I had been questioned once, and my joints still hurt.

I couldn't outrun them. They questioned me in the same way I was questioned before. They didn't get my journal. But they questioned me. They just wouldn't fucking end it.

I ran into my old newspaper reader. He wore a suit now, and he had been selected to help write for the new government. He was exceedingly happy and was already halfway through his first story for them.

"Are we winning the war?" I asked.

"I don't even know if we are still in the war. And I don't really care. If we aren't out of the war, we should be soon. The tsar has abdicated. Abdicated!"

"What does that mean?" I asked.

"It means he has renounced his throne. He is just a man like you and me now."

How could the tsar not be the tsar anymore? "He is no longer the tsar?"

"No, he is a prisoner now. A prisoner of the new government. Just like me. Well, I'm not a prisoner. I just write for them now."

"A prisoner? Will he be executed?"

"There is talk of a trial, but I don't think they will. The tsarist loyalists are still trying to get him back and resist the new government. But I'm sure he won't be in tsarist comfort anymore. You can't abdicate and eat it, too," he said with a laugh. I didn't understand his joke and didn't care. I handed him a new newspaper and some blank paper.

"Thank you, sir, but that won't be necessary. The new government provides my materials now." He rested his hands by gripping the breast of his new jacket. He was almost hugging himself.

"I'll need to find someone else then, won't I?" I asked.

"I'm afraid so. I won't have time. They have ordered two plays and a novel. I have no idea how I'll be able to write fast enough to keep up." He was so excited that he was boiling over like a teakettle. "Now that the oppression is over, the people are hungry for literature, culture and art. But if you ever need any information, come find me."

"Maybe you can tell me something," I said. I took out the silk bastard's lighter and handed it to him. "Do you know what has become of the owner of that lighter?"

He fidgeted with his glasses as he looked at the engraving.

"Ah, yes. After Rasputin was killed, the owner of this lighter was sent to the Persian front lines. Apparently, it was punishment for what he did to Rasputin. That saved his life, though. Most of his family was executed, and his home was confiscated along with the churches. I heard the British smuggled him out."

"Of course they did." I really don't like the British. He held out the lighter for me to take.

"Keep it. It goes nicely with your new suit," I told him. He smiled and hugged me.

I never saw him again. I thought about what he said about the confiscating of churches. I headed toward my old part of the city.

I could see the church from a distance. Since the workers left the factories, there had been no smoke or soot accumulating in the air. I could see the sky, but black ash still lingered like a mist. I came to the church and knocked on the door.

The door creaked open, and the rusty hinges squeaked and sounded like a little girl screaming, "Thank you." This was the first time I had ever been through the front door. There was nothing of real value in the church, but the people took it anyway. They took the wooden crucifixes and the pewter candlesticks. There were dark outlines of where the icons and crosses had hung on the walls; the dirt from the factories never touched these areas. They were echoes. The floorboards had been ripped up for fuel, and all the windows had been broken with bricks.

The priest was sprawled out on the floor next to his broom, buried in ash. They had beaten him with it. I could still see the blood stains on his beard from where I punched him in the nose. The hatred and anger that had led to his beating was so severe that I imagine the people would have eaten him if he had any meat left on his old bones. He was as broken and discarded as his old, crooked broom. The people, for some reason, didn't take the broom. They just left it on the ground in what was left of the church to fade away.

I tried to sweep away the dirt. I didn't know if it was a church anymore. I swept and swept. Then the factories were turned back on, and the avalanche of black began to fall. It was too overwhelming, and I ran. Like a coward.

The House of Special Purpose

Running was useless. I had nowhere to go. They had more questions. I was taken in for questioning. They kicked and beat and raped. They even cut off three of my toes on my right foot. I begged them to stop. They pointed the gun and shot it at me. It was empty.

The former shoemaker, who was now in charge of the new secret police, conscripted me. He gave the impression of a lumberjack who has been asked to fix a pocket watch.

"Just so you and I are clear: I don't need you. You are here only because they think you have value. I think you are a terrorist. An ugly reminder of our oppression. If it were up to me, I would have you executed. If you get in my way, I'll be most disagreeable. You won't like me like that."

"I don't think I like you at all," I responded. They always threaten you with what someone else will do it. He was very upset. He expected me to be frightened and silent.

"What?" That was all he could think to say, and he couldn't manage to make it threatening. "If you ever speak to me like that again, I'll have you shot. Do you hear me?" He began to hit me over the head with his cane. It took all my resentment to keep me from passing out from the pain.

"Yes," I said.

"Good." He handed me his coat and waved for me to follow him.

A special carriage took us to the train station. I wanted to know where we were going, but it made no difference. The only reason he was here was because he had never been associated with this type of work. That means that he was completely stupid, and that's why he had this position.

We boarded the crowded train. There were no seats available, and the former shoemaker turned to me.

"Fetch me a seat."

"They're all full," I said.

"Not my problem," he replied. I walked over to the closest person and put my hand on his shoulder.

"My friend here needs this seat," I said. The old man stood up and limped away. He hardly needed any convincing. He was used to it. We were all used to it. The former shoemaker quickly took the seat.

"The royal family is becoming too dangerous to be left alive," the former shoemaker said. He was hoping that those around him would think he was an official and begin bowing to him. Most were too exhausted to even notice.

"Then why not just execute them?" I asked. I was tired of his posturing. He couldn't answer me. He most likely was just repeating what he heard his superior say, but he didn't know what it meant. He didn't know why they were dangerous. The scary thing is that, for these men, the royal family was dangerous. They were dangerous to their lives and the life of the country, but they didn't know it.

We rode for hours; I couldn't tell how long it was because the train was too crowded to look at my watch, which didn't work anyway. It hadn't ticked since Rasputin returned it to me. The former shoemaker was practicing lifting his head and sitting up straight.

"Where are we going?" I asked.

The dingy cart took us miles over muddy country roads. There were smoke columns of several fires in the distance, and I was eager to not have to be so close to such terrible breath. We arrived at the Ipatiev House.

It was four or five stories tall. The building looked like a church that had been leveled off at the top with a knife. There were only two entrances, and a wooden fence surrounded the compound. All of the posts were of different lengths, and the wood was rotting away.

We were stopped at the gate, and the former shoemaker said something to the guard. After they exchanged a few words, the guard approached me. I handed him my new documents, issued to me by the former shoemaker, and watched him try to read them.

"Do you have a weapon?" the guard asked.

"No."

"Step down here so we can search you." I looked at the former shoemaker who waved me on without looking at me. I jumped onto the muddy ground with a squish. The guard ran his hands over me. He had no idea how to properly search for weapons. He didn't even find my journal.

The former shoemaker called to the driver, and the cart went into the compound without me.

"Okay," the guard said dimly. "You can go on." I had to walk the rest of the way through mud toward the house, which made my foot with the missing toes hurt. The smell of human waste was overwhelming. When they had built the wooden fence, they did not take into account the need for the guards' and agents' waste needs. They were burning the filth, which caused flies and mice to swarm the house. The drone of the flies was so loud that we had to shout to be heard.

"Welcome to The House of Special Purpose," I heard a guard say. They had given the house a new name. I don't know if it was meant as a joke or meant to sound official. Most of the guards had no idea how to fire a gun, and the men in charge were unable to coordinate anything. They were factory workers, farmers and tradesmen. They had no tactical or strategic training and were simply following the chain of command out of blind fear. You can't have someone work under you who isn't afraid of you.

The former shoemaker waved at me as though I had been sleeping on the job. I couldn't walk much faster in the mud, but he didn't seem to care. When I walked up the stairs to the front entrance, he handed me his coat and gloves.

"Take me to the tsar," he said. The guard lifted his rifle from behind his chair and led us into the house. The floor was covered in muddy footprints.

We looked through the window to a table that had been set up in the middle of a small garden. The royal family and their attendants sat and stood around the table. We could see the tsar, the tsarina, the four daughters, the son, a valet and a lady in waiting. Each of them had a shaved head.

"Why did you shave their heads?" the former shoemaker asked.

"They contracted lice."

They looked like skeletons. The tsarina and the daughters tried to hide their heads under hats, but it was easily noticed. The tsar, with his head and beard shaved, looked like he was dying of consumption. I pitied the tsar, but he made his deal with the devil. He kept his son alive in the most unnatural way, and now he was paying the price.

I looked at him directly in the eyes. When he looked back, I was amazed that he was just like any other man. He didn't recognize me. I was just another man to him as well.

This is the same man who sent the entire Russian naval fleet to Japan to be destroyed. He was the man who marched millions to their deaths. He was the most powerful man alive. Now he sat in this muddy garden with no hair, waiting to be fed like a circus animal.

The former shoemaker took his gloves and coat from me. He put them on and went outside. He stood in front of the tsar with his chest puffed up and his hands shaking behind him.

"I am the new commander," he said. "I am a direct representative of the Soviet government." He stood over the seated tsar like a statue for minutes. "The family is to remain in their quarters for the rest of the evening." He had just thought of this order, as a way of demonstrating his authority.

The guards approached, and the family stood up. They walked in a line toward the house without one word. The tsar's son passed by me and stopped. He was the cause of all this. His sickness started a chain of events that destroyed lives and killed thousands. He had no concept of his trespasses. His guilty innocence made me hate him more.

He turned back and walked up toward me. He reached out and buttoned my coat properly, smoothing out the creases with his palm and straightening the collar. When he was finished, he patted my coat, turned toward the house and followed his mother like a little duckling.

End of an Empire

We were at The House of Special Purpose for almost two weeks. There was nothing to do, and we were becoming bored and restless. The former shoemaker spent most of the time in his sitting room alone. He would receive and send messages to his government and smoke anxiously by the window. He spent a lot of his time dodging and hiding from the tsar. Whenever the family was moved, he would shut the doors to his sitting room and not come out until they were out of sight.

I was well-rested and had steady meals. The outside was cold, and the inside was warm. I had freedom to go inside and outside as I pleased. If I became too hot, I could go outside. If I was tired, I could go to sleep. I was given a great deal of small tasks and orders from the former shoemaker. He didn't know what needed to be done, so he invented tasks to validate his position.

Eventually, all the days became one long day. Then, one morning, the former shoemaker received a message and left abruptly. He was gone for many hours and returned with ten men. They looked like they were from the local militia and waited outside behind the fence for most of the day, out of sight of The House of Special Purpose.

Once the tsar and his family had retired for the evening and were tucked away upstairs, the former shoemaker gathered us into the sitting room downstairs. He closed the doors and the windows. The room was not large enough, so we were standing shoulder to shoulder. It was an unsettling feeling to have so many men in a room in complete silence.

He pulled a chair in front of the fire and stood on it. He wanted to appear more official. But he almost slipped and had to grab the shoulder of the man next to him to get steady. He had two men standing outside the door, stomping their feet. He didn't want people outside the room hearing him. He held an important message tightly in his fist.

"The tsarist army is approaching. We can't have the royal family fall back into their hands. At midnight, a truck will be coming," he whispered. It was even more difficult to hear him when he tried to whisper; he was a terrible mumbler. "Once the truck arrives, we will gather the family into a room downstairs and execute them. We will not wake up the family until the truck arrives. Aside from the ten men I brought from the militia, the rest of you should just go about your normal duties and act normal. You are dismissed," he said finally, stumbling off the chair.

It took a few moments for everyone to start moving and breathing again. All their eyes were wide, and they exited the room stiffly and silently. They seemed to wander about aimlessly, as though they were feeling around a new room in the dark.

We waited for hours on that damned truck. I watched the gate through the window as the former shoemaker smoked and drank. He was trying to stop shaking, but the drinking was making it worse. He pushed his lips together and made an odd clicking sound in the back of his throat.

I rested my head on the window to cool off. The more the former shoemaker stoked the fire, the hotter it became, and the more he undressed. The more he undressed, the cooler he became, and the more he had to stoke the fire. I saw some movement outside and finally saw the gas-powered truck. It was large with a heavy tarp covering the flatbed in the back. It was noisy and had a column of smoke coming out the side. The tires and doors were muddy, and it wobbled like a newborn horse.

"The truck is here," I said, taking my head from the window.

"It's about time," he said, anxious to have this night behind him. "Come with me."

He walked slowly upstairs. I almost ran into the back of him a couple of times. Each step he took was slow and deliberate. When we reached the top, he took the lamp from the guard stationed outside the door, paused for a moment and then burst into where the tsar and his family were sleeping.

"We are going to take you and your family downstairs," he said. I watched from the doorway.

"What is this?" the tsar said, still half-asleep. He pulled the covers away from his face and blinked uncontrollably.

"You must wake so we can take you and family downstairs."

"Why?" the tsar asked.

"We can hear mortar fire from the fighting, so we are moving everyone to the basement." The tsar looked at him out of the side of his eye. The former shoemaker shifted his feet and cleared his throat. "We are moving you to a place of greater safety because there is fighting in the town."

"Very well." He propped his body up with his elbows and shook his head to wake up. We should have killed them here, while they were sleeping. It was cruel to wake them only to kill them. It was cruel even to them. Their incompetence made them ever crueler.

The former shoemaker exited the room and thrust the lamp into my hands before stomping downstairs. The tsar swung his feet over the bed and stood. He saw me and slammed the door. The sound made everyone in the house jump. I walked downstairs carrying the lamp.

I heard noises in the basement and followed them. I entered the room where the family was to be taken and saw the former shoemaker looking around.

"This room is too small. We won't have space to use the rifles."

"How much space do you need?" I asked.

"It's too small, you idiot!" he screamed. "Come with me."

We walked back upstairs and into the room where all the weapons and ammo were kept. He opened a crate and took out pistols two at a time. "We will have to use pistols," he said in a wet whisper.

He kept handing them to me. I put as many as I could in my pockets and under my arms. They were cold and heavy. He unlocked the crates with the ammo. He pulled out two small metal boxes of ammunition and shoved them under his arms.

"This way," he said. We entered the sitting room, and he shut the door behind us. There were ten men standing by the fire. They were militiamen and looked like a herd of deer. Most of these men had never seen a firearm. "I want each of you to take one," the former shoemaker instructed.

I handed each man a pistol.

Every pistol I gave away removed a large weight from my pants and back. They each grabbed their pistol as though I had given them a cobra.

The former shoemaker handed out ammunition. The men were having trouble figuring out how -- or even where -- to get the bullets into the pistols.

They couldn't load the ammunition themselves. They were not trained soldiers but angry tradesmen. I had to load the ammunition into most of the pistols myself. My thumbs ached from working the cold, hard metal.

"Keep your fingers off the triggers," I told them. "And point them at the ground, away from our feet." They followed my directions like children. I was worried that they would accidentally shoot me.

"When you see the tsar and his family walk down to the cellar, you must follow us," the former shoemaker said. "Be as quiet and discreet as you can. We don't want to make them panic before we get into the room."

It took them almost an hour to dress themselves and prepare to be moved to the basement. I wondered if they would have taken so long to get themselves ready had they known what was awaiting them. After two in the morning, we received word from upstairs that they were dressed and ready to move to the basement. The former shoemaker and I gathered at the bottom of the stairs and waited for them with the normal guards. The militiamen stood in the sitting room, peeking behind the door.

The royal family descended the stairs as though they were participating in another coronation. The tsar carried his son, who was weak and almost asleep. Behind the tsar followed his wife, four daughters, the family's medical doctor, the tsar's valet, the lady in waiting and the family's cook. They must have all been trained since birth to walk down the stairs together gracefully.

"Follow me," the former shoemaker said, leading them downstairs. We sounded like a herd of bulls marching down the stairs. The wooden frames creaked under the pressure of our weight.

When the former shoemaker came to the room, he stopped and waved the family inside. The eleven condemned people crowded into the small empty room. When they were settled, the former shoemaker counted them with his fingers. Then he exited the room and walked toward the guards and myself. He was searching for a moment or a bell that would sound to let him know when and what to do. There would be no bell.

"We need chairs," the tsar demanded, still believing they were just being held in the basement for the evening. We all looked at each other, wondering if we should bother with it.

"Go fetch some chairs," the former shoemaker told me.

"Really?" I asked.

"Yes!" he said with the confused irritation of an idiot. I walked upstairs and grabbed the first two chairs I could find. I wish I had Rasputin's chair to give him, or perhaps the chair I sat in when I first had my audience with him. I brought them down the stairs, banging the legs into the wall.

I set the chairs down in front of the family. The tsar put his son into the arms of the valet and stood directly in front of them. He took one of the chairs and placed it so the tsarina could sit. Then he put the other chair next to her, took his son back and sat him down.

As I left the room, I passed the former shoemaker. He re-entered with the ten militiamen. They crowded in, standing shoulder to shoulder. Only a couple of feet separated the firing squad from the prisoners.

"Because attempts are being made to rescue them, he and his family are to be executed," the former shoemaker said.

"What? What?" the tsar said. I don't know if he didn't hear the mumblings of the former shoemaker, or he just didn't understand why this was happening.

The shooting started and pinched my ears. Although the men were young and cruel, they were not effective. I could tell none of them had ever shot someone at close range. The black smoke from the pistols created a black fog that circled the small stuffy room. There was some shouting and the rhythmic pop of the guns. Yelling. Coughing. Running. The men ran, coughing out the black smoke and trying to catch their breath.

"The bullets are bouncing off of them," one of them said. Once a few of the militiamen had left the room, I could see the former shoemaker shooting his pistol. He pointed his gun at the tsar's son and fired.

"What's going on?" he asked. He left, trying to reload his pistol. It was too smoky in the room to see anything. He had to push and poke different parts of the gun to try and remember how to load new bullets.

The small boy was still moving and crying. I couldn't believe he was able to withstand such an assault. Once the former shoemaker's pistol was reloaded, he entered and shot the tsar's son three more times in the head. With the boy finally dead, he left the room.

The militiamen had hurried upstairs. Some of them dropped their guns. I looked into the room. There was so much black smoke that it was as though there was a terrible storm in that small cramped space, raining black powder down on the bodies of the royal family.

The wall was painted with black smoke, holes and bright red waves. I was shocked to see movement. Most of the bodies were still moving around, groaning and grunting. The former shoemaker went over to one of the guards and pulled the bayonet from his rifle. He shoved it into my hands. "Finish them off. After that, we'll load them into the truck."

How could ten men at close range leave anything to be finished off? I took the bayonet and turned it properly in my hand. I could taste the powder from the shooting.

I approached the heap of the royal family. Most of them were still moving, their pale faces silently screaming and begging. When I saw the lack of effectiveness of the bullets, I knew the incompetence of the shooters couldn't be completely to blame. I bent over to inspect the wound of the tsar. He was staring at me with eyes that would have fired at me had they not been attached to his head.

I felt his body in the middle of his chest. He let out a scream. I felt small bumps and gaps under his clothes. I ripped open his shirt and saw that his entire vest had jewels and diamonds sewn into it. The tsarina was jerking about next to me. I ripped open her dress and saw that she, too, had sewn diamonds into her corsets. The entire family had smuggled them before they were captured, and they now acted as armor against the bullets.

I picked the bayonet up from the ground. The tsar knew instantly what was happening. But his eyes drifted off as he shook dumbly like a mad man in the street. I didn't want to do anything to them, but I saw the suffering in their eyes begging me to end it. I stabbed him a few times and watched him bleed to death. I was the last person to look him in the eyes before he died.

And now he has nothing.

I had nine more to deal with.

I grabbed the tsarina, stabbed her and moved on. I walked around the room, bent over, stabbing those whom I came upon. The only person they managed to kill properly was the cook. Why did we have to kill the cook? The largest daughter was dead by the time I got to her. I didn't want to kill the next two, but they were in such pain that I thought it wasn't such a bad thing to do.

As I was looking for the fourth daughter, I grabbed some of the diamonds and put them in my pocket. They were like shiny fruit from a dead tree. Then my fingers grabbed onto something that was wooden. I picked it up and wiped away the blood. It was a small portrait of Rasputin. I was so frightened to see his face again that I dropped the bayonet.

"Everything alright in there?" the former shoemaker asked.

"Yes. It's just really messy." I grabbed another daughter and opened her dress. She also had a portrait of Rasputin. Even in this small portrait, I could see his eyes. They were like white attack dogs. I was reminded of his last letter to the tsar. He predicted their deaths. He made a fool of me and cursed me from beyond. I was the fulfiller of his black prophecy. I was the one who killed the tsar and his descendants. His photo was smiling at me. My hands were stained black. I looked at the bloody bayonet and wept. He had won.

    Then I heard a cough. I pushed over a body and found the smallest daughter under a pile of lifeless limbs. I cleared away the dead bodies and put my hand under her nose. She was breathing hard. I pulled her up and ripped open her dress. Remarkably, not one bullet touched her. She had some bruises on her chest and was unconscious, but she was very much alive.

The Future

I wrapped the torn clothes back over her and rested her on my knee. Then I grabbed another body -- I believe it was her dead sister -- and put the corpse on top of her. I still carried my bayonet in my hand. I held it backwards so the blade rested against my wrist, out of sight. I lifted them both up and left the room. The air had a looser grip outside the room. The taste of gunpowder and paint was lodged in the back of my throat.

"Where are we taking them?" I asked.

"There is a truck outside." I didn't see who answered, but I began walking up the stairs. I stumbled back and almost fell over. Halfway up the stairs, I had to stop and rest the two girls on my knee. Their weight was tearing at my old infected knife wound. It was Rasputin, punching me in the side. Rasputin was trying to stop me! I heard someone from the room yell out, "Diamonds!"

The little girl began to shift. I lifted them up quickly and continued my ascent. I pulled a muscle in my chest, and a bloody flap of cloth flew into my mouth. I spat it out and licked the collar of my jacket to get the taste out of my mouth. My side kept tearing. Rasputin was twisting his knife in me. He didn't want me to escape with the princess alive.

When I stepped outside into the cold darkness, there was no order. Men were pacing back and forth, shouting and pointing. They were aimlessly wandering, trying to find direction. There was cannon fire and blasting in the distance. The fire of waste glowed against the dark night.

The cannons sounded like muted thunder and coughing. They were terrible whispers that reminded me of Rasputin's last letter to the tsar. His perverted commandment that declared none of the royal family shall live. It was as though he had put his crooked hand over the country and began to squeeze. Until I saw this breathing girl, I thought he had won. All of my work would have been for nothing. I would have been just another dirty bastard who beats old priests and extorts desperate women. But he hasn't won yet; this child lived. She is the last living descendent of the tsar. She will live and have children, and the tsar's line will continue

This girl's life had been lived at the expense of the misery of countless other children. But I had to keep her alive. I knew she could never grow up to rule Russia. But she could grow up. And then I would have defeated Rasputin.

I put the two girls on the edge of the truck and rolled the lifeless one toward the back. The little girl lifted her head and looked around with bright white eyes. One of the men who passed by grabbed me and saw that I had the little girl with me. I immediately flipped the bayonet around.

He was about to yell, but I grabbed him and stabbed him five or six times as quickly as I could. Then I cut his throat and tossed him onto the pile under the tarp in the truck. They're not organized enough to miss him or careful enough to notice him when they bury the bodies. Although this man died by my hands, it didn't feel like murder. I had no mind to do it; it just happened. All I thought about was keeping this small girl alive.

I wanted to take his shoes, but the soles were in worse condition than mine. I took his coat off and shifted his body under the body of the other girl I brought out. In the corner, he was almost invisible in the dark. I put the coat around the little girl and used the sleeves to tie it in place.

"What is your name?" I asked the little girl. She couldn't respond; she just looked at me. I could taste the sweet smell of the diesel from the truck. It made me light-headed and sleepy.

I took off the left sleeve of my coat and put her under it, holding her up with my arm. I walked with a limp anyway, so this would be the most natural way to walk in case someone saw me. My coat kept slipping down below my collar, and I had to use my other hand to flip it back onto my shoulder. It was not a big problem; I wouldn't be cold until the morning. I waited for a gap in the lines of men wandering about and walked toward the forest.

The new weight caused the knife wound in my hip to bleed down my leg and over the princess. Rasputin was trying to infect her. After I had walked as fast as I could for twenty minutes, I stopped. The house was so far out of sight that I could afford to rest. There was a village thirteen miles or so from here. We might be able to bribe a ride somewhere or buy a horse.

I removed my coat from her head and looked down. She was looking up at me with her bright blue eyes. She was shaking uncontrollably, and her skin was like ice. I was unsure what to do, so I tried to squeeze her tightly. She gasped and held onto me with her thin little arms. Maybe I wouldn't be alone anymore.

"What is your name?"

"Anastasia," she said.